MISSY TARANTINO

Duck Down

First published by Honeybee Publishing; LLC 2022

First edition

This book was professionally typeset on Reedsy.
Find out more at reedsy.com

Contents

Chapter 1 1
Chapter 2 7
Chapter 3 14
Chapter 4 16
Chapter 5 22
Chapter 6 25
Chapter 7 31
Chapter 8 35
Chapter 9 40
Chapter 10 46
Chapter 11 50
Chapter 12 59
Chapter 13 65
Chapter 14 71
Chapter 15 80
Chapter 16 84
Chapter 17 92
Chapter 18 104
Chapter 19 109
Chapter 20 114
Chapter 21 118
Chapter 22 125
Chapter 23 131
Chapter 24 137

Chapter 25 148
Zucchini Pie 152
More Pie? 153
About the Author 154
Also by Missy Tarantino 155

Chapter 1

Hopping onto the driver's seat of the golf cart, I looked in the mirror and adjusted my wig. I thought the short, blond spikes made me look ten years younger than my 67 years. Satisfied that everything was as it should be, I released the brake and headed away from the farm. I loved the paint job that my artistic granddaughter, Quinn, had put on it for my birthday. The red and white stripes along the front and sides looked like they were waving in the wind, and the blue roof with its white stars made me feel so patriotic. Much better than the plain white it had been, that's for sure. It was such a nice day, I had rolled the clear plastic sides up and secured them to the roof. Reaching the dirt road that led to town, I paused and admired the lush green rows of corn that were in front of me. A slight breeze blew and I breathed in the scent of the flowering trees of my orchards.

Bumping over the wooden bridge, I glimpsed the sparkling water of the Paisley River. It was a medium-sized river, just wide and deep enough to provide me and my fellow farmers with irrigation water and the townspeople with a recreation area. In fact, I was convinced that the clear water from our river was the secret to my sweet apples.

I turned left onto Main Street and headed towards Something Nice, the local coffee shop. At this early hour, there was very little traffic. My sleepy little town was just beginning to wake up. I could have made my own coffee at home, but I was craving one of Nora's pastries. She is a truly gifted baker. It was going to be a busy day and her food was just the ticket for giving me the energy I needed. Plus, the added benefit of catching up on a little of the town gossip, of course.

The street curved around Paisley Point's crowning feature, its graceful park. It reminded me of a jewel set in the center of a ring. The beautiful old stone business buildings faced toward the park across a street that was paved with red bricks. Offset to one side of the park was a large lake with a heart-shaped island that functioned as a sanctuary for a flock of wild birds.

I left the golf cart near the park's pavilion, in front of the statue of the town's founder, John Paisley, and crossed the street. The bell over the door jangled as I pushed it open. The heavenly scents of freshly brewed coffee and cinnamon buns rushed at me.

"Good morning, Granny!" Nora smiled from behind the counter and held up a large white mug. "Want a cup of Joe?" Nora was middle-aged, slim, and had rosy cheeks from her hot ovens. Her auburn hair was tied up in a bun at the base of her neck. Her shop was filled with eclectic odds and ends for decorations. A shelf filled with old watering cans, tin signs advertising baking powder, a flower wreath on the door. I think I read in a magazine somewhere that it was shabby chic. I called it homey.

I nodded and perused the glass-fronted case of pastries that Nora had freshly baked. "I think I'll have a bear claw, too."

"Good choice," came a deep raspy voice behind me.

Turning around, I looked at the man wearing dirty blue coveralls and a stained green ball cap sitting in the corner. He was holding up his own bear claw in a large, weathered hand. Earl Foxman owned the farm next to mine and had been coming to town for his breakfast every morning since his wife had passed away several years ago. I smiled and nodded, wanting to be friendly, but not wanting to encourage conversation. Talking to Earl could be a challenge.

When Nora had filled my cup, I picked up my food and walked towards a seat by the front window, overlooking the park. "Here, come sit with me," came Earl's voice, followed by the sound of a chair moving across the tile floor. "No sense in us both sittin' alone this mornin'."

Not able to think of a plausible excuse not to, I changed directions and sat at Earl's table in the proffered chair. He cleared his throat and started in. "You notice all them washboards on the road by your place? The county's not doin' their job of maintainin' the roads. Those things are getting mighty deep. They's caused by folks driving way too fast. If the dang law enforcement don't start settin' speed traps out our way, they may as well just turn it into a drag strip." He paused to take a loud slurp of his coffee.

I nibbled on my pastry, suddenly losing my appetite. It was too early for this nonsense. If I had heard this speech once, I had heard it a thousand times. Earl had a very short list of topics of conversation. This particular gem was number three. I glanced at my watch and mentally set a ten-minute timer. I could endure this monologue for that long. I think.

The bell jangled and Corrie Wagner, the town's recreation director, walked in. Dressed in her customary pink polo shirt and white shorts, it wasn't hard to see why she won the town's Cross Fit competition every year. She was wearing a golf visor and had her dark brown hair pulled up into a short ponytail. Her two children were with her, a boy who looked to be about eight, and a girl no older than 6. Both were sporting backpacks and school uniforms.

Corrie marched up to the counter and said, "Two milks, a vente coffee with non-fat milk, and three sausage pockets to go." She waved her hand in a dismissive motion and reached into her back pocket for her phone.

"There's trouble," Earl muttered to me in his deep gravelly voice.

I nearly choked on my breakfast and shifted uncomfortably in my seat. True, Corrie wasn't the most tactful person, but I didn't appreciate being the recipient of Earl's kind of gossip. I was more the 'guess who's having a baby' kind of gossiper. I *really* didn't enjoy being caught in the middle of one of his famous spats. He would probably pick a fight with a porcupine over who had the right of way.

Corrie directed the two children to a table across the room. Then she strode over to our table, her neck muscles bulging. "I heard that. Just what were you referring to?" She jutted out her pointy chin and glared at him. I could see a vein on her forehead throbbing.

Earl slowly took another slurp from his mug. "Oh, nothin'. Just don't see how puttin' that much money into a competition's gonna benefit this town any." He gave her a stony glare and wiped his mouth with a napkin.

Corrie clenched her teeth. "We went over this at the board meeting the other night, Earl. I thought you had all your questions and concerns addressed there. When the vote came through, all but one director thought this was a great idea. I wonder where the dissenting vote came from? If you want to bring more business to this little backwater town, you've got to make it worth people's while. You are just too tight-fisted to realize that you are hurting this community." Corrie had been hired a few years ago from out of state. I didn't know much about her, but sometimes new blood can be good for a place to keep bringing in fresh ideas. I knew that if Earl had his way, Paisley Pointe would have been turned into a time capsule.

Earl turned his attention to me. Great. So much for staying out of things. "What do you think, Granny Appleton? Do you think this little shootin' match is worth the $25,000 this gal's costin' the town?"

I glanced at Corrie and noticed another vein standing out on her forehead. I hate it when Earl makes people uncomfortable. I sat up straighter and said, "I happen to think it's a wonderful idea! I've even entered myself in the competition." I patted my hair and looked at my watch. Two minutes to go. I could feel my blood pressure rising. "I don't think there's any harm in a little competition, to be honest."

"We'll see," Earl said, narrowing his eyes. "You better watch yourself, Corrie. As I recall, your evaluation's comin' up before too long. I don't like your attitude." He looked at her over the edge of his coffee mug. I could feel the tension rising as they stared at each other.

Corrie opened her mouth, then shut it into a tight line. She turned on her heel and walked back to the counter. She paid for her food, gathered her children, and headed for the door. The kids walked outside and she paused. "Don't light the match if you don't have the fuel for the fire, Earl," she said, shooting daggers with her eyes. Flipping her ponytail over her shoulder, she marched out the door.

"If that woman has her way, this town's gonna be overrun with tourists traipsin' through, makin' a mess, ruinin' our quiet little town," Earl said, swallowing the last bite of his bear claw. He draped his arm over the back of his chair. I recognized the position. He was getting ready to launch into another lecture.

I set my mug down and before my brain had time to stop me, I said, "Seems to me, Earl, that she's trying to make this town better. These businesses need customers. Where do you suppose the money's going to come from for your speed traps and road graders? How deep are your pockets? Are you going to fund it all?" Out of breath, I stood up and took my mug back to the counter. I don't know if my two minutes were up, but I couldn't take anymore.

Before Earl could reply, I headed for the door. Once on the sidewalk, I paused to compose myself. That man could push my buttons faster than I could dial a telephone. I felt a little bit ashamed at how I'd spoken my mind but figured he needed to hear it from someone.

Chapter 2

Sitting in my golf cart, I tried to collect my thoughts. That interaction between Earl and Corrie had rattled me. Not the way I wanted to start my day. I reached under the edge of my wig and pulled out a slip of paper. Opening it, I ran down my list of errands. First off was a visit to the beauty salon, True Colors. I needed Priscilla to do a refresh on my white-blond movie star wig. I figured it would give me a boost of confidence on Friday for the archery competition. Tucking the paper under my wig, I drove down the block.

On my way around the circle, I passed a white truck with the Paisley Pointe logo on the door. The driver waved as she passed. I waved back and smiled. It was my granddaughter, Quinn. She had moved in with me over the winter when Ricardo, her ex-boyfriend and NYC art critic, had published a very unfavorable review of Quinn's work. She was shunned out of galleries and had lost all confidence in herself. She had landed the job of groundskeeper for the town and was thriving in our little community. I just wished she would get herself out on the dating scene again.

Priscilla's shop was in one of the oldest buildings in town. It had a stone façade and large windows facing the street. As I walked in, six pairs of eyes turned to greet me. One pair belonged to Priscilla herself, who smiled and said, "Be with you in just a minute, Granny." She stood at one of the three hairdressing stations, painting color onto her customer's hair and covering it with strips of foil. Her own blonde hair was piled high on her head in a beehive, held in place with sparkly pink combs. She was wearing a pink tank top that accentuated her large chest. Her flip-flops showed off hot pink toenails.

I nodded and waved as I walked over to the small seating area and sat on one of the comfortable chairs around a low coffee table. The shop definitely matched Priscilla's colorful personality. The walls were painted a vibrant shade of yellow and were covered with posters advertising outlandish hairstyles.

Peeking out from under the foil was one of my good friends, Divina Bloom, who happened to own the flower shop in town. She waggled her fingers in my direction. "Good morning, Granny. What are you up to today?"

I held up my market bag. "Just dropping off a wig for a wash and fluff," I said. "I want to look my best on Friday for the archery competition. I have a feeling I'll need the confidence boost. I'm on my way to my first practice session after this. You are never too old to start a new hobby, I say."

Divina gasped. "I didn't know you were competing! How exciting! I'm creating a lovely bouquet for the winner. I hope it's you." She clapped her hands and set her foils moving.

The other two stylists added their well-wishes, too. They were busy with clients, who had their backs to me. I glanced in the mirror to see if they were anyone I knew. One of them was a stranger to me, but the other one looked very familiar. It was a young woman in her twenties with a petite face and long neck. She was thin and had large, doe-like eyes framed in dishwater blonde hair.

I stared at her reflection for a moment, then exclaimed, "Judy Foxman, is that you?"

The woman stepped down from the chair as the stylist finished her haircut. "Hello, Granny. It's been a while." She smiled shyly. Her pale skin was set off by the royal blue top she was wearing.

I crossed the room and enveloped her in a big hug. She was at least a head taller than me. "I just came from the café, and your father didn't say a word about you being back in town. It's so good to see you. You haven't been home in what, two… three… years?"

"I just got here and haven't been out to the farm, yet. I wanted to look my best before I go and face the old codger." She smiled and opened her wallet to pay her bill. "You mean three years since he kicked me out. He didn't like the fact that I wanted to pursue dance as a career and told me not to come home until I'd found a real job." Little spots of pink appeared on her cheeks. She swallowed and said, "I've come home to show him how wrong he was." There was a glint in her eye that told me that she was done being pushed around by her father. Oh, to be a fly on the wall for that conversation.

"How long are you in town? My granddaughter is living with me now. Do you remember Quinn? We'd love to have you and your dad over for dinner sometime."

Judy shrugged and tucked her wallet back into her designer bag. "I'm not sure how long I'll be here. Depends on how long it takes to knock some sense into his thick skull. We've got some old business to take care of and I'm not leaving until he hears me out. Wish me luck." With that, she kissed me on the cheek and walked out, waggling her fingers to Priscilla.

I turned to Priscilla, who shrugged her shoulders. "That one has a lot of pain in her life, I'd venture to guess." She held out her hand and gestured for my bag. After getting confirmation that the wig would indeed be competition-ready before Friday, I left the shop.

I made my way back to the great expanse of lawn that made up the majority of Paisley Park. A group of people was setting up easels with targets on them and marking off lines for distances. I spotted Corrie lugging a large trashcan one-handed across the grass. The can was full of arrows with feathers in a rainbow of colors. One of her assistants was wheeling a rack of bows right behind her. I felt my hands start to tingle. This was going to be fun. I had never been into archery but was willing to try anything once.

I joined a group of bystanders and said hi to a few of them. When everything was set up, Corrie called us together. She unwrapped a mint and popped it into her mouth, tucking the wrapper into her pocket. "OK. Let's get started." Her nasal voice sounded like a bullhorn. "Since all of you are new to this, let me explain what we have here." She pointed towards a group of targets. "The three smaller targets are 80 centimeters across. We call them faces. They are for the two closer ranges we are going to shoot: 30 and 50 meters." She gestured to another set of targets. "The three larger targets have 122-centimeter faces. They are for shooting the longer distances of 70 and 90 meters."

A shadow crossed the grass. Corrie scanned the sky, muttering, "Stupid birds," under her breath, then continued. "The object is, of course, to hit the bullseye in the center. That will get you ten points. But you get points for hitting the other rings as well. For today, I'll just be happy if you hit the face." We all laughed. She didn't.

"I have a whistle," Corrie said, holding it up. "This is important. When you hear two whistles, that's your signal to approach the line." She blew twice and we watched her assistant walk up to the white chalk line in the grass holding a bow. The quiver was slung over her shoulder and hung low behind her back. "When you hear one whistle, you may shoot." She blew the whistle and we watched the assistant nock an arrow, aim, and let go. A loud thunk indicated she'd hit the target.

She turned back to us. "You'll shoot six arrows at a time. That's called an 'end'. When you hear three whistles, you may walk downrange and collect your arrows. During the competition on Friday, you'll have an official who scores your points, then you'll mark your arrow holes with your initials before returning to the staging area behind the line." We heard two more thunks as the assistant fired more arrows at the target.

Corrie raised her voice another notch. "If at ANY point you hear FOUR whistle blasts, that means there is imminent danger and everyone should stop what they are doing. It could mean anything from a timing error to a person crossing the field of fire." By now, Corrie was pacing back and forth in front of us with her hands clasped behind her back. She reminded me of a drill sergeant. All she needed was the hat and boots. "Are there any questions?"

She paused and gave us each the evil eye. I shook my head and so did everyone else. Even if I had a question, I didn't want to be singled out. She might make me drop and give her twenty!

Next, Corrie counted us off into three groups. Each member of the group chose six arrows from the trashcan, making sure that no one in the group had the same color of feathers – er, fletching, I learned they are called. We picked out a bow from the rack and had a lesson on how to stand with our feet apart, how to nock the arrow onto the bowstring and aim down the arrow shaft at the target. I felt like I was back in junior high school, which was probably the last time I ever shot an arrow, to be honest. And I'm not going to tell you how long ago that was. Corrie used her own custom set of arrows and bow for the demonstration.

When it was time for my group to step up to the line, I tried my best to remember all the directions. I managed to hit the target with two of my six arrows, but the other four fell pathetically short of the mark. I was waiting for the all-clear whistle to sound when the woman next to me started walking down the grass towards the targets. Four loud whistle blasts sounded right behind me, causing me to drop my bow.

"Stop where you are!" Corrie bellowed. "Isla Marsh, what do you think you are doing?"

The woman turned around and looked at Corrie in alarm. "I was just going to get my arrows," she said, meekly. She pointed at the target. Like we didn't know where the arrows would be.

Corrie stomped over to her and took her by the arm. She led her back across the line and scolded her. "You HAVE to wait for the signal! You could have been struck by an arrow. Don't do that again." She dropped Isla's arm and walked away, muttering under her breath. I watched as she popped another mint into her mouth.

Poor Isla was shaking. I put my arm around her shoulders and said, "No harm, no foul. You're fine. Just wait for the rest of us next time. We'll go together, OK?" She nodded her head and brushed the tears off her face.

Hearing three whistles, we all walked down toward the targets, picking arrows from the field as we went. I giggled to myself. I'm glad I wasn't the only one who missed their target. I had been worried that I would be the only one not experienced in archery.

Back at the line for my next try, I nocked my arrow, aimed, and let go. Thwack! I was as giddy as a schoolgirl. This was so much fun. I was concentrating so much on repeating my success, that I didn't notice the flock of ducks flying over us toward the lake.

Suddenly, in the midst of the familiar sound of arrows striking targets, came a new sound. A high-pitched quacking, followed by a loud thump. Four whistle blows sounded and everyone froze. Something caught my eye. Something was moving in the grass next to one of the targets.

Chapter 3

Two seconds after the all-stop whistle sounded, everyone dropped their equipment and ran downfield. Corrie, with her unnecessarily muscular legs, was the first to reach the target. She stopped suddenly and spread out her arms. The crowd reached her position and stopped.

My short, stubby legs just couldn't keep up. By the time I made my way to where everyone was standing, I was huffing and puffing like a dragon with COPD. Pushing my way to the front, I saw Corrie and her assistant standing in the grass next to a beautiful male mallard duck, who was alternately struggling to flap his wings and pulling at its feathers, sending the soft down feathers floating everywhere. I noticed a bright blue band around one of his legs. A long, black arrow with bright yellow fletching protruded from one of its wings.

"What do we do?" someone in the crowd asked.

Another person piped up, "Do we call 911?"

"Who's arrow is that?"

If there's one thing that I cannot stand, it's an animal in pain. I looked around the group. No one seemed to know what to do. Well, I did. Spotting a young woman with a light jacket tied around her waist, I walked over and said, "May I please borrow your jacket?" The girl quickly untied it and handed it to me.

Holding the pink jacket in front of me, I approached the duck from behind and gently laid the coat over its body and head. I folded the uninjured wing against the duck's body and picked it up. The duck struggled and quacked loudly. "Everybody move! This duck needs medical attention right now!" The crowd parted like the Red Sea and I quick-stepped to my golf cart. I could hear people behind me but didn't pay them any attention.

I held the duck against my body with one hand and steered with the other. I could feel the mallard's heart beating through my shirt. I released the brake and reversed out of the parking spot. Hearing tires screeching, I looked in the rear-view mirror. A large black truck with oversize tires and a lift kit was sitting cock-eyed in the middle of the street. I only caught a glimpse of the driver, who was leaning out the window, shaking his fist.

Throwing the cart into drive, I took off like I was trying to make up time after a pit stop in the Indie 500.

Chapter 4

Pulling up in front of the Harp Street Vet Clinic, I punched the brake and slipped off the seat, trying not to jostle my new friend. Having its head covered had helped to keep it calm. The glass door wouldn't give when I tugged on it. Grunting in frustration, I speed-walked around to the back of the building. Doc's big diesel truck was just pulling into his reserved space in the alleyway. The bed of the truck was filled with stainless steel boxes and kennels.

I stood by the back door and watched impatiently as the vet gathered his belongings and stepped out. "What's up, Granny?" He squinted at me through his thick, black glasses. His nose was peeling and there was stubble on his chin.

"A mallard duck took an arrow through the wing during archery practice at the park," I said. I glanced down at the pink jacket and saw the duck's legs sticking out at the bottom.

Doc's face grew serious and he fished his keys out of his pocket. I followed him into the cool darkness of the storage room. The smell of antiseptic and animal waste hit me hard. I live on a farm and am used to lots of odors, but this was intense. I wrinkled my nose and hurried past the noisy kennels and cages holding current patients.

We went into an examining room and I gently placed my

squirming bundle on the stainless-steel table in the center. Doc peeled back the jacket. Up until that point, the duck had made very little noise. As soon as his head was uncovered, he started quacking up a storm. He snaked his head out and would have bitten Doc Worthington's hand if he hadn't had lightning-fast reflexes. The scars on his hands showed just how many opportunities he'd had to practice this particular skill. There were no fresh scabs, so I'd say he was getting pretty good at it.

"Easy there, fella," he said calmly as if seeing ducks struck with arrows was an everyday occurrence. He took the jacket the rest of the way off and handed it to me. I promptly threw it behind me onto a chair. Whistling, Doc said, "This doesn't look good. Can you hold down his other wing, so I can examine him?"

I nodded and put my hands around the mallard's body to hold it still. I was surprised at how scrawny it was, under all those feathers. Doc pointed at the blue ring around the duck's leg. "Ah-ha! It's the Blue Banded Bandit. You're famous around here, little guy." He grinned at me. "You know about this bird, don't you? He lives on Heart Island. He loves shiny objects and will steal anything you don't keep an eye on. He took my best spinner out of my box one day when I was fishing for carp in the lake. He would have taken my pole, too, if it hadn't been too big for him."

Quinn came home from her job as the town's groundskeeper with stories of people chasing after a duck and having to rescue items it had taken. I had seen him do it several times but didn't know that he had a nickname. "The Blue Banded Bandit, huh? Say that five times fast." I looked at the little guy with renewed interest. "I guess today he was just in the wrong place at the wrong time."

Doc turned on a bright overhead lamp. Starting with the wingtip, he used his fingers to feel along each of the bones. The closer he got to where the wing joined the body, the louder the duck quacked. It was shaking, too. I murmured, "It's OK, little guy. Doc won't hurt you. You're going to be fine."

Doc Worthington was the only vet in town and everyone loved him. A month ago, I had brought in a stray cat that had been hit by a car at the end of my driveway. The cat's injuries were too severe and Doc had had to put it down. Tears streamed down his face while he eased the animal over the rainbow bridge. I may or may not have joined him in the waterworks.

Not only did he tend to everyone's pets, but Doc also made the rounds of the farms in the area. He came out to my place regularly to check on my animals. I have a sneaking suspicion that he likes to sample my pies, too. Doc is an avid fisherman, too. I'm guessing that the peeling nose was from the fishing trip he'd taken the weekend before with Earl Foxman. I knew that they were good friends, but for the life of me couldn't figure out what they had in common.

"Hold onto him, Granny. I'll be right back. I've got to go out to the truck and grab some tools." I watched him go, noticing how his shoulders stooped a little. He soon returned holding a leather carpenter's belt filled with hammers and chisels and other woodworking implements.

I raised my eyebrows and tilted my head. "Are you going into construction, Doc?"

He grinned and explained, "When I'm out doing my farm rounds, I never know what I'll run into, so I have to be prepared for anything." He set the bag on the table and took out a pair of wire cutters. "Sometimes animals get stuck in fences. Hopefully, these are as good at cutting arrow shafts as they are wire."

He instructed me to cover the duck's head with the jacket to help keep it calm, then gently turned the duck on its side. With one hand, I held the duck down. With the other, I held the injured wing away from its body. I noted the soft brown of the duck's belly, and how it contrasted with the darker feathers on its back. There was a band of deep blue on the wings that I hadn't noticed before. I was always amazed at the variety of colors in God's creatures.

"We should give him a better name. Any ideas?" Doc asked, maneuvering his cutters.

I shook my head. "Maybe we should call him Dennis the Menace after all the trouble he's caused."

The vet studied the mallard for a second. "Nah, Dennis doesn't fit him. I think he looks like Harvey."

"Harvey it is," I agreed. We smiled at each other over the table. If I tried to count how many times I'd stood in this exact place with an injured animal, we'd be here all day. Doc may be an old softy, but so am I.

Doc gripped the arrow and clamped the wire cutters down on the shaft as close to the wing as he could. The shaft of the arrow was about as big around as a pencil and was painted black with orange bands on it. The fletching on the back was neon yellow. With a loud snap, the arrow shaft broke. The mallard paddled its feet in the air and quacked frantically.

Laying the arrow on the table, Doc said, "That was the easy part. Now we have to pull this arrow out. I'm not sure if it is in the bone or not." He looked at me anxiously. "You doing OK? I guess I should have asked you that before we started."

I had helped Doc with other minor procedures here at the clinic and also at the farm, so I wasn't feeling queasy or anything. I had been so focused on the duck's discomfort that I hadn't considered my own. "I'm just fine, Doc. Don't you worry about me. You just focus on this little guy right here."

With a small smile and a nod, Doc turned and pulled some gauze, latex gloves, and other materials out of a cabinet on the wall. Then he rummaged in the carpentry belt and pulled out a pair of pliers. After getting everything sterilized, he injected some local anesthetic into the area around the arrow. "Hold him tight, now. This might require some muscle." I braced my legs against the table and Doc gritted his teeth. Harvey voiced his objections to the plan. Doc took a deep breath and gripped the shaft of the arrow on the back of the wing. He pulled and twisted at the same time. The arrow didn't move.

Doc changed positions and took another grip. "That sucker is really stuck." He pulled again, with no result. The drake paddled his feet in the air weakly. Shaking his head, Doc said, "I'm going to need to x-ray this to see if it is completely through the bone." He glanced at his watch. "We'll have to wait for my staff to get here. I'll make him comfortable in a crate until then. You go on about your day and I'll call you when we get this out." I started to protest and Doc held up his hand. "I know you want to help and believe me, you are a great assistant, but this is probably going to require surgery. I'll keep you in the loop, I promise."

Disappointed, I held the door open while Doc picked up the duck. I left the clinic only after watching the little guy through the door of the cat crate for a solid five minutes. I took the discarded jacket and went through the supply room and out the back door to the alley. Only then did I remember that I'd left the golf cart parked out front. Sighing, I put my head down and trudged around the building.

Hearing someone clearing their throat, I looked up to see that my trusty golf cart was blocked in by a big black truck, and a large man with a red face was leaning on it, with his bulging arms crossed. A tattoo of a skull dominated his forearm.

Chapter 5

"Can I help you?" I asked, crossing my own arms. I stopped and looked at the man. He was at least six feet of solid muscle under a tight black t-shirt and form-fitting gym shorts. He sported a military fade haircut and had a long white scar on his jawline.

The man pushed away from the golf cart and started walking toward me. "Yeah, you can help me. You can explain why you jumped out in front of me and almost made me wreck my truck."

I put my hands on my hips. "Watch your tone, young man," I said, more bravely than I felt. "I don't know what you are talking about."

The man raised his voice and pointed a meaty finger at me. "I had to slam on my brakes, old woman. You made me spill my coffee all over the front seat of my truck." He was gesturing wildly. "Now you're going to pay for cleaning it." He advanced a few steps closer.

I sidestepped until I was in front of the glass doors to the clinic. I knew that they were still locked, but I also knew that Doc was inside. As loud as I could, I said, "You'd better watch it, Bub. There are folks around here that don't take kindly to strangers roughing up their senior citizens." Behind me, I could hear keys in the lock.

The door opened and Doc stepped out, holding a cell phone to his ear. "What's going on, Granny? Who is this?"

"Some hot-under-the-collar meathead," I said. I could feel my knees quaking in my jogging pants. "He was out here when I came around the building." I moved over closer to Doc, wishing I was holding the hammer from his construction belt.

Jock man took a step closer to us, his fists clenched.

"Hold up, buddy," Doc Worthington said. He held out his free hand. "I heard the ruckus and thought we could use some help here. The police are on their way."

"Perfect!" the man shouted waving his arms. "They can write her a ticket for reckless driving and get her to fix the damage she caused." He was spitting while he talked and pointing that finger at me again.

A white patrol car with the Paisley Point logo on the door pulled up behind the black truck. A young officer in a short-sleeved uniform stepped out. The big man turned and stomped toward him.

"That old woman is a menace!" he yelled, jutting his chin in my direction. "She jumped the curb right in front of me over on Main Street. I nearly wrecked my truck."

The officer tilted his head to look around the man. He pointed at me. "That woman?" A smile teased the corners of his mouth.

"Do you SEE another woman? Is everyone in this hick town stupid?" the man said. He waggled his head as he spoke and swept his arms out wide.

"Good morning, Doc. Good morning, Granny," the officer said, ignoring the gyrations. He sidestepped the man's arm and walked towards the building.

Officer Lance Baird was fairly new to the force in Paisley Pointe. Of course, 'new' in this town could mean anything from one day to twenty years. If my memory served me right, I thought he'd been here about three years. All the young women in town swooned over the handsome officer, whom I knew to be unattached. I made a mental note to invite him over for dinner soon. He would be a perfect match for Quinn. Yes, Officer Tasty might be just the ticket. Oops! Pun not intended.

Officer Baird turned to the red-faced windmill and said, "Can I talk to you for a second?" He motioned for the man to go with him over to his vehicle.

Doc put his arm around my shoulder. "Granny! You are shaking like a leaf!" he exclaimed. "Are you OK?"

"Adrenaline dump," I said calmly. "That guy is lucky you showed up when you did. I was ready to try out some techniques from my self-defense class at the rec center." I glanced over at the black truck and saw the man give his driver's license to Baird. At least he wasn't screaming at me anymore. Taking a deep breath, I could feel my body returning to normal.

The door to the clinic opened from the inside. "Hey, Doc, there's a call for you." Eryn McLaughlin, the young, petite secretary, gawked at the man in the tight t-shirt. "Who's that?" she asked, pointing with a long, bright red nail.

"Nothing you need to be concerned about," Doc said. Turning to me he said, "Are you going to be alright?"

"Right as rain," I said, smiling brightly. "Thanks for being my knight in shining armor. Keep me posted on Harvey's condition."

Doc took Eryn by the shoulders, turned her around, and said, "Let's give these folks some privacy. We've got a ton of work to do, anyway."

Chapter 6

After Officer Baird took my statement and accepted an invitation to dinner next Saturday, I hopped into the golf cart and eased off the brake. I drove sedately down the street and around the corner. I went the long way around our circular main street, checking every intersection twice. Deep down, I felt like that black truck was lurking somewhere, just waiting for a chance for a showdown.

Spotting Quinn's groundskeeper truck parked by the boathouse on the backside of the park, I thought I'd stop by and see how her morning was going. And not tell her about her dinner date next week.

The boathouse was more like a shed that also doubled as a pump house for the automatic sprinkler system for the park. Water was pumped out of the lake to water the grass. Walking around the corner of the boathouse, I could hear Quinn talking to someone inside. I stopped in the doorway and knocked, not wanting to interrupt.

"What do you want?" came Quinn's gruff voice.

I stepped into the dim building. "I just came to say hi." I looked around. "Who were you talking to?"

Quinn shook her head, her thick blonde hair flying around her face. "No one. Just cussing out Lucy Cantana in the privacy of the boathouse. She can be so frustrating. Also, I swear I locked the boathouse when I left on Friday. When I got here this morning, it was unlocked. I can't wait until this tournament is over and things get back to normal. I think I'm losing my mind." She blew a stray piece of hair out of her eyes.

"What did Lucy do to you?" I asked. Lucy Cantana had a reputation in town as being more than just a little difficult to get along with. She was not one you wanted to cross. It was no wonder that the local restaurant and watering hole, Pointe of No Return, had hired her as a bouncer as well as a bartender.

"She didn't do anything to me," Quinn mumbled. "I'm just swamped with work and now I have to stop everything and run over to the island because that stupid duck stole her keys. Apparently, yesterday she was in the park, playing Frisbee with her dog. The duck took her keys right out of her pocket. He has a thing for shiny objects. When she called me, she was beyond mad. I'm not looking forward to facing her when I find her keys. She sounded like it was all my fault. Like I'm supposed to control the wildlife around here."

"She'll get over it. Lots of folks have had something taken by the mallard, from what I hear. Even Doc." I laughed. "One time, before you came to live here, I saw that duck waddling across the grass with a knitting needle in its beak with a little old lady hot on its tail. She couldn't catch him."

Quinn laughed. "I can picture that! That duck is worse than a crow. He's been known to have quite a collection out on that island. I'm sure I'll find some interesting things out there. Luckily Lucy was able to catch a ride home yesterday with a neighbor."

"Want some company?" I asked. "I'm curious about what else that duck might have taken."

We grabbed the oars and headed down to the water's edge. We flipped the boat over and pushed it into the water. Rowing out to the island, I admired the view. The water was still and glassy. The birds were chirping and the air was fresh. Early April in Paisley Pointe was picture perfect.

"This is the mallard that has the blue band on his leg, right?" I asked. For all I knew, there were several mallards with klepto tendencies on the lake.

Quinn said, "Yes, each one of the permanent resident ducks has been banded a different color so that we can tell them apart. Everyone calls him the Blue-banded Bandit."

"Oh, well, you should know that I took him to Doc Worthington's this morning. As we were practicing our archery this morning, someone accidentally shot him in the wing." When Quinn gasped, I hastened to add, "Doc is going to take x-rays and remove the arrow. I'm sure the duck will be fine. He promised to call me when it's done." As an afterthought, I said, "We changed his name to Harvey."

"That fits him to a T," Quinn laughed. "A little prim and proper, and a little loud-mouthed." She dipped her oars into the water and sent us skimming across the water.

We landed the boat and pulled it up onto the shore. Stepping out, I looked around. I'd never been on the island. It was small, covered with tall grasses and willows. There were also two old cottonwood trees with gnarled branches in the center of the island. It was called Heart Island because of its shape. The section of the bank closest to the boathouse cut in, like the top of a heart. If the bushes hadn't been there, you could probably cross the entire island in 20 steps. With the willows, however, the interior was difficult to navigate.

Quinn said, "There are at least three nesting sites, hidden

under the willows. The females are nesting this time of year, so let's try to avoid those areas. They are used to humans, so we probably won't frighten them, but better safe than sorry."

She led the way around the shoreline to one of the cottonwoods. "There's a hollow log around here where Harvey likes to hide treasures." We found the log easily. It had once been a large branch on the tree, but a terrible windstorm had torn it off ages ago. One end of it was about ten inches in diameter. Quinn knelt down to check inside. "You've got to see this, Granny. Harvey has been busy."

I got down on my knees and peered into the hole. Inside was a pirate's booty. I pulled out a silver spoon, an earring, and a baby's pacifier. No car keys, though.

"His other favorite spot is on the opposite side of the island," Quinn said. We went back the way we came and around the shoreline on the opposite side of the island. I could feel the warmth of the sunshine on my shoulders. Spring is my favorite time of year. The colors, the smells, the new life. I couldn't wait to see the baby ducks following their mamas around the lake. Pausing a moment, I took in the beautiful park that was Paisley Point's pride and joy. Quinn was doing a great job as a groundskeeper. The flower beds were coming alive with tulips and daffodils, the shrubs were trimmed and the grass was the color of an emerald.

A meandering stream, lined with cattails, flowed across the oval-shaped park and into the lake from the west. It left the lake on the south end, rejoining the river on its way to the ocean. Quaint bridges graced the stream, offering romantic photo opportunities for newly engaged couples. A large white gazebo stood proudly on an expanse of grass, surrounded by lilac bushes that were in full bloom. Catching a waft of their scent, I paused and breathed deeply.

Catching up with Quinn, we found the other hiding place. It was a low spot under a pussy willow bush. Its branches were covered in the soft pinkish gray buds that gave it its name. Quinn gently moved the branches aside. Looking over her shoulder, I saw a small nest, lined with duck down in the hollow space close to the trunk. There, in the center were the missing keys! They were attached to a key chain with a charm hanging from them. The charm was a beer mug with froth spilling out of the top. The letter 'L' was embossed on it. When Quinn picked them up, something else caught my eye. A shell casing. From a gun. Now, where in the world would Harvey have found that?

A shrill whistle came from the opposite shore. I looked up to see a giant of a woman standing there. She wore black bicycle shorts and a tight yellow top. When I say big, I don't mean fat, I mean tall and muscular. She was unbuckling a helmet as she stared across the water at us. A fancy race bike with think tires leaned against her hip.

"Did you find my keys or not?" she yelled.

Quinn held up the keys and jangled them. "I've got them right here."

"Took you long enough." Her loud, brash voice attracted the attention of everyone nearby.

Instead of answering, Quinn turned around to face me. "Could you take them to her? I really don't have the time to listen to her rants today." Her big blue eyes pleaded.

"I'll handle Lucy," I said. "I may even give her a piece of my mind about her attitude." I took the keys and put them into my pants pocket. We walked back to the boat and paddled back to the boathouse.

Quinn gave me a big hug and went back to work. I squared my

shoulders and drove the golf cart around the lake to where Lucy was waiting, tapping her foot. I smiled to myself and used my age to my advantage. I looked in the mirror, adjusted my wig, and slowly slid off the seat to stand next to the cart. Placing one foot carefully in front of the other, I walked up to Lucy.

"Good morning, Lucy. Beautiful day, isn't it?" I could see the tendons in her neck tighten.

Lucy shifted her weight and showed her teeth. I think it was an attempt at a smile. "I guess so. Now, where are my keys? If I could have caught that duck, I would have wrung its little neck. If he tries it again, he won't be so lucky."

I pulled the keys out of my pocket. Lucy reached for them, but I pulled my hand away. "Just a moment, if you please. You catch more flies with honey, you know, Lucy. Maybe try saying please."

"PLEASE may I have my keys, Granny Appleton?" Lucy said between clenched teeth.

I held them out. "That's better."

Lucy snatched them from my hand, spun around, and stomped off with her bicycle.

Watching her march away, I whispered, "You're welcome." There was something completely unsettling about that woman. It wasn't just that she was taller than the average woman, or thicker. It was more than that. It had something to do with the way she looked through you like she wanted to steal your soul. I shook my head and thought, *There's something going on with that one. She's certainly been hurt at some point in her life. That bravado is a cover-up for hurt.*

Chapter 7

I pulled out my phone and checked for messages. Doc had said he would call me, but maybe he'd forgotten. There was time for me to run over to the vet clinic to check in on poor Harvey before going home to make lunch. Quinn had left home extra early this morning and I was sure she had skipped breakfast. I wanted to make sure I had something extra tasty for her to eat.

Jumping into the golf cart, I drove across the grass and onto the street. Out of nowhere, a big black pickup pulled onto the street behind me. I pulled to the curb to let it pass. The driver honked his horn and waved as he drove by. It was Sterling Springer, the mayor of Paisley Pointe. Since when did he drive a big black truck? I waited a minute to let my heart come back out of my throat and return to where it belonged.

At the clinic, the smell of caged animals and antiseptics continued to be overwhelming. I had heard somewhere that if you breathe in through your mouth, smells weren't as bad. Whoever had said that was lying. Not only could I still smell it, but now I could taste it, too. I walked up to the reception desk to talk with Eryn.

"What's up, Granny? Who was that man in the parking lot this morning?" Eryn asked.

I shook my head. "I have no idea. Some Mr. Atlas wannabe

with anger issues. I stopped by to see how that mallard I brought in was doing." Eryn was quite the spreader of little stories, and I really didn't want to get involved in it.

"Let me see if Doc is free." Eryn rolled her chair back and walked through the door dividing the waiting area from the rest of the clinic.

I sat down on one of the wooden benches to wait. Across from me was a bulletin board covered with business cards and notices about pooper scooper services, groomers, missing animals, and other pet-related announcements. Next to that was an industrial shelving unit stocked with different animal foods and cat litter to purchase. A poster advertising worming medicine decorated the wall next to the door. It reminded me to check if the farm cats were up to date on their immunizations.

The door opened and Doc Worthington strolled into the room. He smiled at me and motioned for me to follow him. "Our little patient is doing great. We had to use general anesthesia on him to get that arrow out. Just as I suspected, it went into the bone, narrowly missing a major artery, too. He's one lucky duck." He chuckled. "Get it? Lucky duck?"

I gave an obligatory laugh. Doc was always trying to crack jokes. Half of them, I didn't understand, but I think it was mostly in the delivery. We stopped in front of one of the hospital cages and looked inside. The mallard sat there, looking at us with sad eyes. His head drooped and his wing was bandaged with white gauze and tape. More gauze secured the wing to its body.

Doc turned serious and said, "He's having trouble coming out of anesthesia. He'll perk up soon. I'm afraid he'll never be able to be released back into the wild. The wing was so badly damaged that he'll never be able to fly again. Which means he'll be vulnerable to predators. If we let him loose back on the lake, a fox might get him."

In my mind, I was thinking, *Or an angry bartender.* "Do you think he'd get along with domestic ducks? I could take him to the farm."

Doc slapped me on the back. "I was hoping you'd say that! It's worth a try. Nothing ventured, nothing gained, I always say."

After getting detailed instructions on wound care, we put the duck into a cat carrier and deposited Harvey on the floorboards of the golf cart. "Quinn will be happy to see you," I said to the duck. I was always adding to my menagerie of misfits.

When Quinn strolled into the kitchen for lunch, I was just pulling a pie out of the oven. I set it on a rack next to another one I'd made earlier.

She gave me a hug and a peck on the cheek. "It smells heavenly in here."

"Thank you! And I brought a friend home, too." I gestured to the cat carrier by the door.

Quinn chuckled. "One of these days, I hope it's a person, not another animal. What is it this time? A mother cat and her kittens? A potbellied pig?"

I smiled to myself. I almost spilled the beans about Officer Baird's upcoming visit. "It's Harvey, the duck," I said. "That arrow damaged his wing. I brought him home to live with our domestic duck. Doc says he won't be able to fly and can't go back to the lake or he'll be some critter's dinner."

Quinn knelt down and peered inside the carrier. "Hey there, fella. Welcome to the farm."

"Are you OK waiting a few minutes for lunch? I need your help creating a pen for our new friend." I wiped my hands on a kitchen towel and headed out the door.

In the barn, we created a small enclosure out of chicken wire close to the wall, using the large stack of hay bales as the back of the pen. We filled the interior with straw and set a large shallow pan of water in one corner. Our two farm dogs, Wags and Brock, watched curiously from the doorway. We filled another pan with chicken feed and slid the big barn doors closed, leaving the duck to settle into its new surroundings.

When lunch was over, I said, "Would you mind taking one of these pies over to Doc on your way back to work? I owe him at least that much for his help this morning." I boxed it up and sent her on her way. Maybe I should have sent her with another pie for our handsome young Officer Baird, too.

Before we went to bed, Quinn and I went to the barn to check on Harvey. A stray nail on the door snagged my shirt. After carefully extricating myself I followed her to the corner.

"How's -," I started but stopped when I saw Quinn put a finger to her lips and shake her head. She pointed to the pen. I tiptoed closer and smiled at what I saw. There, nestled in the straw, was Harvey, but he wasn't alone. Lying next to him, with her long neck stretched over Harvey's back, was our white domestic duck, Peeper. I guess that answers the question of whether he would get along with the flock.

Chapter 8

On Friday morning, I got up extra early to take care of the morning chores. When I checked in on Harvey and Peeper, they were contentedly sitting together in their enclosure in the barn. I refilled the water container and gave them more food. Searching the perimeter, I located the small hole that Peeper had used to squeeze inside. I used some zip ties to close it off so predators couldn't get in. Finally, I tried to inspect the gauze dressing that Doc Worthington had placed around Harvey's wing. Neither of the birds seemed to mind my presence, which shocked me. Peeper was used to me, of course, but Harvey was a wild animal. Strangely, with Peeper around, he was very calm and acted like he'd been with people all his life.

The bandage was still secure and there wasn't anything seeping through it. As I knelt in the straw, Harvey quacked at me quietly and tried to grab the pendant that I was wearing. "No stealing, Harvey. You are a guest here, and in recovery," I admonished him, smiling. It was good to see that he was starting to feel better.

When I stood up to leave, both ducks waddled after me. I slipped through the make-shift gate and quickly closed it up. Peeper and Harvey stood there, looking at me like I was abandoning them. "I'll be back later, I promise." As I closed the big barn door, I could see that they were still standing there, staring at me. Feeling very guilty, I closed them in.

There was chaos in the park when Quinn and I arrived. Barricades had been set up, blocking off the parking spaces facing the grass for the food trucks. From tacos to coffee to pizza, there was something for everyone. Looky-loos drove slowly down the street, creating traffic snares. I drove my golf cart up onto the sidewalk, earning some dirty looks from drivers. My mouth was watering. I smelled cinnamon. Following my nose, I found the source of the sweet goodness. A small pink food truck sporting images of cinnamon rolls took up space close to the registration tent.

Parking next to the tent, Quinn went to handle some last-minute details and I made a beeline for the order window. I waved to the woman inside who wore her hair in a kerchief the way they did in the '50s. Her bright red lipstick and horn-rimmed glasses completed the look. "What can I get you, honey?" she asked, smacking her gum.

I studied the menu on the side of the truck and selected something called a donut-hole sundae. Along with cups of coffee, I carried the sweet breakfast towards the picnic tables under the striped blue and white awning. The sun was beginning to warm the air and dry the dew in the grass. Speaking of grass, I cringed when I thought of how much work it was going to be for Quinn to fix the damage caused by all the tent poles, tables, and foot traffic this weekend.

Quinn joined me and we shoveled bites of cinnamon sugar-coated goodness into our mouths. I closed my eyes. It was like being transported to heaven.

My reverie was broken by the shrill sounds of a woman screaming. Jumping up from the table, we raced towards the sound. A second sound pulsed in my ears with a steady rhythm. Sudden recognition stopped us in our tracks. Quinn changed directions and I huffed after her.

We ran to the golf cart and Quinn jumped into the driver's seat. She threw it in gear and took off at high speed. I was thrown back in the seat. "I forgot to shut off the timers on the automatic sprinklers! I'm such a dolt!" Quinn said, leaning forward. She drove quickly across the area designated for the competition, getting us our second shower of the day. When we reached the pump house by the lake, Quinn unlocked the door. Throwing a switch, the waterworks stopped. I watched the people on the lawn wringing out their clothes. Quinn joined me and groaned.

"Hey, let's drive over to the recreation center and see if Corrie needs any help getting any last-minute equipment loaded up," I suggested. Quinn glanced in the direction of the angry people and nodded.

"Good idea."

We drove around to the storage building behind the rec center and found Corrie trying to wrangle the 122 cm targets into the bed of her blue truck. The actual targets with their bright yellow, blue, and red circles were already loaded. It was the stands that were causing the trouble. They looked like the easels that painters lean their canvases on, only giant-sized. The legs were collapsible and kept swinging around as Corrie tried to lift them.

"Here, let us help," Quinn said, running over. I followed more slowly. After all the running we'd done already, I had a stitch in my side. Besides, I wasn't sure what help I could be with those awkward pieces.

Corrie blew her short, dark bangs out of her eyes. I could swear I saw tears in her eyes. Corrie reached into her pocket and pulled out some mints. She offered one to each of us. They were white and wrapped in clear cellophane. "Thanks for the help. These buggers are giving me the business this morning. I really need this event to be a success. The mayor was hinting that maybe someone else should do my job. That stupid farmer, what's his name? Earl something? He keeps complaining to him. If I lose this job, I'm going to have to pull my kids out of school and go live with my parents in Oklahoma." She unwrapped her mint and popped it into her mouth.

She climbed up into the bed of the truck while Quinn and I lifted the stands up to her. In no time, we had the load tied down, ready to take to the park. As we closed the tailgate, I noticed a bumper sticker that said "My kid can beat up your honor student." Classy.

A big black truck turned into the parking lot and pulled up next to us. My blood froze. It was the big angry man from yesterday. I grabbed Quinn and pulled her around the far side of Corrie's truck. I knelt down like I was tying my shoe.

"What's going on?" Quinn hissed, trying to peek over the hood of the truck.

"I'll explain later," I whispered back. I really wasn't trying to eavesdrop, but I couldn't exactly NOT hear what they were saying.

"Good morning, Nick," Corrie said.

"Here. This is for you. Don't share it with anyone," came Nick's deep voice. I heard what sounded like a paper bag rustling as it changed hands.

"Are you coming to the archery tournament today?"

"Nah. I've got a two-hour workout planned and then some business to attend to. Archery's for wussies, anyway." Nick paused. "Hey, that's the golf cart that almost ran me off the road yesterday. If I catch that broad, I'd like to wring her neck."

Quinn's eyes got big and her mouth tightened.

"Who? Granny? She wouldn't hurt a flea."

"Well, she owes me detailing on my truck. If you see her, tell her I'm coming for her." The door slammed, the truck roared to life and peeled out as he left the lot.

I stood up and came around the truck. I patted my wig nervously. "Do you know that guy?" I asked Corrie. My guts were twisted in a knot and the donut hole sundae felt like a rock in my stomach.

Corrie nodded. "Yeah. That's Nick Zeppa. He's new in town. He's bulking up for some weight-lifting competition. He works out here just about every day. I'd like to hitch my wagon to his star if you know what I mean." She wiggled her eyebrows.

"What did he give you?"

Corrie reached for the handle on the driver's door. "Oh, nothing. Thanks for helping me load those targets. See you at the park." She slipped inside and started the engine.

I stood there and watched Corrie leave. Then I hurried to the golf cart. I didn't want to stay at the rec center and risk seeing Nick again. I could hear his words ringing in my ears.

Chapter 9

"Care to fill me in?" Quinn asked as we followed Corrie back downtown. I didn't want to but knew that I should. So, I told her about my little adventure with the bully yesterday, with the least amount of detail possible.

Quinn said, "That guy is a classic case of 'roid rage. Be careful, Granny."

I patted her hand and smiled. It was so nice to know she cared.

It was amazing the number of people who were milling around the tents and the food trucks. Quinn and I helped set up the targets and found some extra extension cords for the electronic scoreboard. This was turning into a large-scale event.

I walked over to the registration tent and picked up my official number. Then I went to the equipment tent and selected a bow, six white arrows with blue fletching, and a quiver. I felt nervous and excited at the same time. Blue had been my husband Chet's favorite color. Maybe it would bring me luck today. This was my first time competing in something so physical. Usually, I baked some pies and left them on a table to be judged when I wasn't around. That type of competition was much less stressful.

There were so many competitors, that they had to split us into two groups. This was going to be a two-day event. I was put into the second group, to my relief. That way I could watch and see how to do things without embarrassing myself too much. I noticed that poor Isla was in group one. I hoped she would remember to wait for the signals today.

Soon the sound of whistles and the thwack of arrows hitting targets filled the air. The spectator stands were full and the high school cheerleading squad was on hand to pump up the crowd. I stood on the sidelines and watched, in awe of the concentration it took to control their eyes, hands, and breath. It reminded me a little of the golf tournaments my husband used to watch on television. The crowd would be hushed while the archers were setting up their shots. As soon as the arrows struck the targets, shouts and clapping ensued, unless someone made a huge error. In that case, the crowd offered sympathetic groans. Today's competition was the qualifying rounds. Tomorrow was the single-elimination championship, with the winner taking home the hefty prize.

Before I was ready for it, my group was called up by the sound of two whistles. I stood on the line between two strangers. I looked down the line and recognized several local people, some of which had been in the practice sessions during the week.

The sound of a single whistle startled me and I jumped. Everyone around me had already nocked their first arrows and was beginning to shoot. We were only given two minutes to shoot our six arrows. I reached quickly into my quiver and pulled out an arrow. It got caught on the edge of the quiver and I tugged harder. The arrow came out but pulled another one with it that fell to the ground. *Great way to start,* I chided myself.

Biting my lip, I notched, aimed, and let my first arrow fly. It managed to hit the face of the target but was well outside the point rings. Grabbing another arrow, I tried again, remembering to take a breath and blow it out before letting loose. This one did better, hitting the outer ring and earning me three points. The next three arrows completely missed the target. Picking my last arrow out of the grass, I managed to make it into the blue ring for five points.

When I unstrung my bow, the man on my left put his hand on my shoulder. "First competition?"

I nodded, feeling my face flush.

"Don't fret it. Happens to all of us. You'll get the hang of it." The whistle blew three times and he headed downrange.

I followed after him, picking up arrows as I went, and signed my initials next to each of my holes after the judge scored my points. From the stands came encouraging calls from my friends. I could see Priscilla's beehive standing above the crowd. I managed a small smile and a wave.

By the time we had finished all twelve ends of six arrows each, I was hot and tired. My head itched under my movie star wig – which wasn't giving me the confidence boost I had been hoping for. My arm was sore and so were my fingers. In all of our practices, we hadn't ever shot that many arrows. During the lunch break, Quinn brought me a pulled pork sandwich from one of the food trucks. We sat in the shade of the refreshment tent.

"I am so proud of you, Granny," Quinn said, sitting on the picnic bench beside me.

Taking a big bite of the juicy barbecue sandwich, I nodded and smiled. "Thanks, Quinn. I guess I've still got a few adventures left in these old bones after all." I couldn't give my granddaughter a hug, what with holding my messy lunch, so I settled for bumping elbows with her. We chatted about the competition and watched the crowd around us.

As we were finishing up, I heard shouting coming from the

other side of the tent. I recognized that bellowing voice.

"I don't know what you are talking about. Don't touch me! This is your last warning!"

"I saw you with him. Don't deny it, Lucy. I saw you and so did a bunch of other people. Back off. He's mine."

I stood up to get a better look, wiping the last of the barbecue sauce from my lips. Lucy Cantana was holding a white cup. She was facing Corrie Wagner, who was poking Lucy's shoulder with her finger. The crowd had moved off a little to get out of the way of the argument.

"He's NOT my boyfriend. But if I want to work out with him, it's none of your business, so YOU back off."

Corrie shoved Lucy backward. "Stay away from him!"

Lucy threw the contents of her drink in Corrie's face and stomped off. Corrie stood there and screamed, "You'll regret this! Just you wait." People rushed to her side with paper napkins.

With the excitement over, everyone returned to their own business, which in this small town meant comparing notes on what they had just seen and adding in any details they knew about the backstory. If they didn't know any details, they invented some.

The afternoon portion of the competition was even further out of my comfort zone. We were shooting at the 122 cm targets set 70 and 90 meters away. The closer targets had been hard enough, but to shoot something that was a football field away was impossible for me. After attempting six arrows and having all of them fall short of the target, I was ready to give up.

The same gentleman who had encouraged me in the morning was shooting right next to me again. He looked to be about my age, so he was an old geezer, too. "Just relax your shoulders," he told me while we were waiting for the first shooting group to finish their end. "You have to aim a little higher to account for the distance. Not much, but a little. You'll get there." He gave me a grin and I noticed how white and straight his teeth were. I wondered if they were real. *He's not bad to look at,* I thought to myself. He was of average height with short, salt and pepper hair. His skin was tanned from spending lots of time outdoors, not that orange-y look of a fake tan. I looked at his hands and was pleased to see that they were rough and calloused from work, not smooth and soft like a desk jockey would have.

With my confidence restored, I took his advice. I shot my best and managed a respectable score in the next round.

As much as I wanted to stick around and socialize after the competition ended for the day, I knew I needed to get back to the farm and check on Harvey and the other animals. It was about time to feed. Rounding up Quinn we headed for home.

When I slid the barn door open, I waited for a second for my eyes to adjust to the cool, dim interior. What I saw brought a smile to my face. Harvey and Peeper had cuddled up again, with their heads resting on each other's backs.

Peeper had been an Easter present to some little girl, whose family thought that a duckling was adorable. Which it was, but they don't stay that way. When Peeper started to grow out of her yellow fuzzy baby feathers, the family decided to get rid of her. By putting her in a box. On the side of the road. Quinn had found the half-grown bird last summer when she had come to see me for a weekend.

I had fed the half-starved duckling and nursed it back to health. The name Peeper came from the fact that she never developed the iconic quack that ducks have. The loudest sound the duck ever made was a soft peep. Peeper had shown her gratitude by being my shadow any time I stepped foot outside the house. She had even figured out how to use the cat door and now came and went as she pleased.

Seeing the two ducks, one dark and one light, cuddling together, made me smile. Of course, Peeper would want to be a part of this! She had natural mothering instincts and would be the best medicine for Harvey.

The only trouble was, that Peeper wasn't exactly gentle. She was a bit of a train wreck, to be honest. She would trip over her own webbed feet walking on a flat floor and fall on her beak. She wasn't very good at grooming herself, either. The feathers on the top of her head never lay in the same direction. They always looked like she had just rolled out of bed. For a split second, I worried that Peeper would unintentionally harm Harvey by trying to protect him. But as I watched the two ducks, Harvey adjusted himself to get closer to Peeper. Maybe a little mothering was just what he needed.

Chapter 10

When I woke up on Saturday morning, my right arm was so sore that I had a hard time putting my shirt on. The more I used it, however, the better it felt. By the time Quinn and I had completed our rounds with the animals, it was almost back to normal.

"Are you ready for round two?" Quinn asked when we sat down for a quick breakfast.

"Oh, yes. It's going to be even more fun than yesterday. Today we have the single-elimination rounds. They'll take our scores from yesterday and rank us from highest to lowest. We get matched up to compete head-to-head until there are only two shooters left, bracket-style." I took a swig of my coffee. I just hoped that I had done well enough yesterday to not earn the distinction of being dead last. I do have a little ego.

Quinn looked at me over her own mug. "You were sure getting cozy with that guy next to you." She grinned and winked.

I adjusted my wig and patted it in place. "He was just helping me out." I hoped I would get the chance to at least talk with him again today, but I wasn't about to tell Quinn that.

"Sure, he was," Quinn teased, putting her empty dishes in the sink. I guess the matchmaking gene runs in our family.

We drove to the park and I headed straight to the equipment

tent, while Quinn went off to solve an electrical issue for one of the vendors. There was tension in the air among the competitors that seemed out of proportion to the day's event. I sidled up to Isla as she was selecting her arrows. "What's going on around here that has everyone on edge? Did I miss something?"

"Someone slashed Lucy's tires last night. I think we all know who did it."

I grabbed my gear and went to look for Lucy. I found her sitting in the area that had been roped off for the competitors where they could watch when they weren't shooting. Lucy was adjusting a leather arm guard strapped to her left arm. What a smart idea! I kept forgetting to turn my wrist so that the bowstring didn't chew my arm to pieces. I sat down next to her. "I just heard about your car, Lucy. I'm so sorry. Are you doing OK?"

There were dark circles under Lucy's eyes. Her mouth was set in a thin line. "Sorry to be rude, but I'd rather not talk about it. I need to win this money now more than ever, so I need to get my head right and focus."

I took the hint and wandered off to the registration tent. I found that of the 64 entrants, I was ranked 60th. Lower than what I was hoping for, but at least I wasn't in last place. That distinction went to Isla Marsh. The board on the easel showed me competing against a person named Teddy Schneider. I had no idea who that was, but if I beat this person, I would continue to compete. If I lost, I was finished for the day and out of the money. The money didn't matter to me, I had entered the competition for the excitement of trying something new.

I sat in the roped-off section when the competition started and watched pairs come and go. When my name was called, I stepped forward into the area behind the shooting line and strung my bow. Standing next to me, prepping his equipment, was none other than the gentleman who had been so kind to me the day before.

He grinned and said, "So, we meet again!" He reached out his calloused hand and shook mine firmly. "Best of luck to you, madam."

I fumbled with my bow and dropped it in the grass. I reached down to pick it up and all my arrows fell out of my quiver. I was scrambling to retrieve them when I heard the two-whistle signal to step up to the line.

Teddy and I battled it out for five ends of three arrows each, alternating turns with each shot. Teddy shot smoothly and calmly. I watched his technique and tried to copy him. I managed to keep my arrows on the target faces, but Teddy won each end handily.

When we finished our round, Teddy again shook my hand. "Nice work. You are improving." His baritone voice tickled my spinal cord.

I said, "You, too. I mean you did a nice job, not that you need improving." I reached up and patted my wig. "Good luck on your next round." I hurried to my seat in the competitor's box and pretended to tie my shoe. I certainly looked the fool on that exchange!

The day wore on. The sky was a clear blue and the air was still. I started to feel drowsy, sitting in the sun. I decided to get some water from the refreshment tent. The crowd was even larger than it had been yesterday. It looked like the whole county had turned out. *Take that, Earl Foxman,* I thought, *look at all the revenue this event is bringing to our town.*

I entered the tent and there was Earl, sitting at one of the tables with his daughter. A young man was sitting with them.

He looked very familiar, but I couldn't place where I'd seen him before. I wondered if he was part of Judy's plan to show her dad that she had made something of herself. He didn't look like someone you would see in the dance world, but what did I know. Earl was wearing his customary blue coveralls and greasy green ball cap. I grabbed a cup of water and went to sit with them. "I was just thinking about you, Earl," I said. "Look at all these people, bringing money to Paisley Pointe. Eating in the restaurants, buying merchandise, staying in our hotels."

"Bringin' in the wrong kind of people," Earl growled. "There'll be graffiti on our walls by mornin', you mark my words. They's slashin' tires and doin' drug deals, is what they's doing." He stood up. "I just busted a guy sellin' dope out of his big black truck down the street. You tell me how this is good for our town." With that, he stalked out of the tent with Judy and the man following in his wake. I hadn't even gotten around to saying hi to them.

Chapter 11

When I emerged from the tent, I walked down the row of food trucks. Each one of them seemed to be doing good business. I sniffed the air and my stomach growled. I stopped at one called "Hog Wild" and ordered some macaroni and cheese with bacon. The warm gooey snack hit the spot. I took my paper boat and stood in the shade of a tree to eat it.

I really enjoy people watching and there wasn't a better place to do it than an event like this. People from all walks of life strolled around the park. There were couples with young children, teenagers, seniors like me, and tall muscular bodybuilders who said that "archery is for wussies."

I stared at Nick Zeppa. What was he doing here? I took a step back, deeper into the shade of the tree, and watched him. He was standing by himself, leaning on the side of a taco truck. He kept checking his watch and looking around. He took his cell phone out of his back pocket, scrolled through it, and put it back. Another gargantuan man approached and the two of them walked away, behind the line of food trucks. Where were all these large guys coming from? I took one last bite of my food and threw it in a nearby trash can. I walked quickly to the taco truck and peered around it. The two men were crossing the street.

Trying to look nonchalant, I followed them. By the time I'd crossed the street, they had disappeared around the corner. Picking up my pace, I was practically sprinting when I reached the edge of the building. I turned the corner and ran headlong into Nick's six-pack chest. I bounced off and landed on my derriere.

Nick sneered at me and said, "Watch where you're going, old broad." He stepped around me and kept walking. The other man was nowhere to be seen. As I struggled to my feet, he stopped and turned around. "Hey, you look familiar. You don't drive a red, white, and blue golf cart, do you?"

I shook my head and wiped my backside. "Nope. Must be some other old broad." I patted my hair and walked past him towards the park, trying not to limp. I'd never been so happy with my wig collection.

Seeing Officer Baird standing next to the registration tent, I made my way over to say hi. And get information. Maybe.

"Officer Baird, how are you?" I asked brightly. "Enjoying the competition?"

The handsome young officer looked especially nice today in his freshly pressed uniform. It looked like he'd just stepped out of a calendar. He smiled, showing his perfect teeth. "It's a great day. How about you? I heard you were competing."

I pretended to look sad. "I'm out. There are too many good archers here today. But it looks like some of our local talents are holding their own."

"Lucy Cantana could win it all," Officer Baird said. "She's the best we've got."

I agreed. "If she can keep her head in the game, she will. Too bad what happened to her car last night. Any leads on who slashed her tires?" I looked up at him hopefully. Another perk to my age is that people liked to confide in me. I turned on all the charm I could muster.

"None yet, but I have my suspicions," he said. "Lucy will come through. She's one tough gal. You know she's a bouncer, right? Not much can rattle her."

A cheer broke out from the stands. "Looks like another win for Paisley Pointe," I said. I left Officer Baird standing there and went off to watch the rest of the competition. And try to find some ice for my aching tailbone.

When it was time for the final match, the crowd had swelled to the point that it was standing room only. I was very happy to have a front-row seat in the competitor's box. Standing side by side, waiting for the judge's whistle to approach the line, were Lucy Cantana, and the man who had been so helpful to me, Teddy Schneider, who I found out was from Paisley Pointe's rival town of Kirby.

Two short whistles sounded and the competitors stepped up to the line. The judge pointed at Teddy to go first. A single chirp of the whistle. The crowd was hushed as he pulled the bowstring back against his cheek. He released it and immediately came the sound of the arrow striking the yellow bullseye. Everyone clapped politely.

The announcer's voice came over the speakers, "Ten points."

All eyes turned to Lucy, who was prepping for her first shot. Her hands held steady and she pulled firmly on the bowstring. Thwack.

"Ten points," came the calm voice. The crowd cheered. No question about who they were rooting for here.

Teddy pulled a white arrow with green fletching from his quiver and notched it. He took a deep breath and blew it out through his mouth. Then he let the arrow fly. Just outside the bullseye in the red circle.

"Nine points."

Lucy notched her second arrow. It was black with neon yellow fletching. In the silence, I could hear the sound of traffic on the interstate highway outside of town. A gust of wind came through the park just as Lucy released the arrow. It contacted the target solidly in the red zone. Nine points. The score was tied.

I glanced across the grass at the spectator stands. They were packed with Paisley Pointe townspeople. Standing next to the ropes, I was surprised to see Nick Zeppa. For a guy who didn't like archery, he sure was intent on watching the competition. Then I noticed who was standing next to him in her pink polo and white shorts. Corrie Wagner was holding onto Nick's arm. You would think that the director of the town's recreation center would be happy that one of her own people was in the finals, but the expression on her face said otherwise. *If looks could kill*, I thought to myself. I pulled my attention back to the competition.

Teddy pulled his final arrow from his quiver. He squinted at the target as he raised the bow into position. I clasped my hands together and held them to my lips. A big breath in through his nose and out through his mouth. His shoulders relaxed and he released the bowstring.

"Nine points." A nervous murmur erupted along with polite clapping from the crowd. The pressure was building. If Lucy made a bullseye, she would win the competition.

Lucy wiped her forehead and shifted her weight. She selected an arrow from her quiver and ran her hand down the black shaft. She kissed the neon yellow feathers for good luck.

Arrow notched, bowstring pulled, eyes glued to the target. Lucy paused, then released the arrow. The crowd gave a collective gasp, then erupted into cheers. Lucy had done it! A perfect bullseye, dead in the center.

Madness ensued. People rushed onto the grass. Competitors surrounded Lucy, hugging her and patting her on the back. The cheerleaders led the crowd in a victory cheer.

When order had been restored, Lucy stood on the announcer's platform. Mayor Springer congratulated her and handed her a trophy and a giant check for $25,000. The crowd went wild for a second time. Lucy grabbed the microphone from the stand and said, "Let's meet at The Pointe of No Return and celebrate!" She held the trophy over her head. There were tears streaming down her cheeks.

Wally Teller, the local radio host was standing nearby, waiting to get an interview with the winner. I made sure to give him a wide berth. There was just something unnerving about hearing yourself on the radio.

After going back home to do chores and change clothes, Quinn dropped me off in front of the restaurant and returned to the park to help with cleaning up. I waved to her as I opened the door. The restaurant and bar were crowded and the music was loud. I don't particularly like country music, but it certainly fit the theme of this place. There was wooden paneling on the walls with stuffed animal heads for decorations. The railing around the dance floor was made of wagon wheels. I managed to squeeze my way to a table that faced the dance floor just as the people occupying it left. I ordered a soda from a waitress wearing a cowboy hat and sipped it as I watched couples twirling around, having a good time. Most of the dancers were doing a line dance in the middle of the floor. I spotted Priscilla's tall blonde hair. She was dancing with a gentleman in a tall black cowboy hat. They sashayed past me going around the perimeter of the floor. It reminded me of the roller skating rink where I used to take my son when he was little. Everyone skated going in the same direction.

Someone came and sat down next to me. I turned and gasped, "Why, Divina, don't you look nice!" My friend, the florist, was decked out in a western shirt with fringe along the sleeves and rhinestones everywhere. Her newly styled hair was short and blonde, streaked with low-lights.

"You don't think it's too much, do you?" She had to lean close because the music was so loud.

I shook my head. "Not at all. Not for this place especially. Any special reason for the fancy duds?"

Divina blushed. "Well, since you asked, yes. It's our anniversary!" Divina was married to Mayor Springer. "And I'm going to drag Sterling out on the dance floor whether he likes it or not." She was patting her hand on her knee in time to the music.

Sterling appeared holding two drinks. He sat down across from Granny. "Hello, Ms. Appleton. I would have brought a drink for you, too, had I known you were here." He was decked out in a black button-down shirt with red piping across the front, forming two V shapes. His shirt was tucked into dark blue jeans which sported a belt with a large silver belt buckle.

I held up my soda. "I'm fine, Sterling. Drop the Ms. Appleton stuff. You know I don't like standing on formality."

He grinned playfully at me and held up his own glass. "Here's to a successful tournament!" They all toasted the weekend. Diagonally across the dance floor, they could see Lucy standing in the midst of a crowd. Sterling said, "Don't let anyone know I said this, but I sure am glad that one of our hometown people won."

Divina stood and tugged on Sterling's arm. "Come on, Cowboy.

You promised to dance with me tonight. I didn't get all gussied up to just sit here." She stuck her lips out in a pout.

Sterling stood up and bowed to his wife. "Ma'am, may I have the pleasure of this dance?" He extended his hand and when she placed her hand in his, he kissed her knuckles.

Giggling, she followed him around the wooden divider. I watched them, smiling. A single tear dripped down my cheek. Seeing the happy couple made me miss my late husband, Chet. A dull ache settled in my chest. Feeling a tap on my shoulder, I turned to see Earl Foxman standing there. He had changed out of his dirty blue coveralls and was looking quite spiffy in a gray dress shirt and clean blue jeans. He was still wearing his green ball cap, though. I was feeling a little under dressed in my flowered blouse and black slacks.

Earl was smiling and holding out his hand. I shook my head and tried to wave him off. He nodded and held out his hand a second time. Not wanting to be rude, I allowed him to lead me out to the dance floor. Just then, the DJ started a slow song. *Great,* I thought, *just what I need. People starting rumors about me and Earl Foxman.*

Earl turned out to be quite a good dancer. He led me around the dance floor and even got me to do a few twirls as we made the rounds. By the time the song ended, I was actually enjoying myself. As the last strains of the music played, Earl bowed to me and escorted me off the floor. I blushed at the attention and patted my wig, making sure it was still in place.

We made our way over to the bar and asked for something to drink. I had never liked the taste of alcohol, nor the feeling it gave me, so I stuck with soft drinks and water. Earl ordered the local craft beer. We found some empty bar stools and perched there to watch the crowd. I was half hoping that my fellow competitor, Teddy Schneider, would make an appearance. Being from our rival town and coming in second place, I doubted that he stuck around.

I turned to put my empty glass on the bar. When I turned back around, I was faced with a painted-on black t-shirt over a well-sculpted chest. Looking up, I saw the beefy neck and red face of Nick, the body-builder. He was puffing up his chest as he talked to Earl. In one hand he was holding a glass of beer.

"Look, old man. I know it was you that sent the cops after me. You'd better back off and mind your own business if you know what's good for you. I know where you live."

Earl slowly stood up and faced Nick. He only came to Nick's chin, but he puffed out his chest, too. "I don't like you, son. I've been watchin' you, ever since you showed up around here. You ain't been exactly an upstandin' citizen, what with your big loud truck, and whatever secret stuff you been sellin'."

There were only about six inches separating the two men. The music blared and the dancers moved smoothly by. It was as if they were a little island in a fast-flowing stream. They stared at each other like they were each waiting for the other one to make the first move.

"I've got as much right to be here as you do," Nick spat. "Next time you try to get in my way, I'll bust you up!"

I was getting nervous. Neither of the men was on my most-liked list, but I couldn't stand by and let this happen. I stood up and felt suddenly aware of just how short I was. Not letting that deter me, I made a wedge with my arms and forced the two men to step back. "Now, just hold your horses. This is a party. Let's not spoil the mood here. You'd best leave if you can't be civil."

Nick took his free hand, put it against my face, and pushed me aside. At the same time, he threw his glass on the floor and swung a fist at Earl's face. I went flying back against the bar. Earl ducked and jabbed Nick in the nose. With a roar, Nick charged at Earl, grabbing him around the shoulders, bearing him to the ground in a football tackle. With the wind knocked out of me, I could only gasp for air and watch the two men wrestle.

A group of men rushed over and pulled the fighters apart. Nick's nose was bleeding and his skin-tight shirt was torn, revealing a well-formed pec. Earl's shirt had come untucked and he'd lost his green cap. The line between his tanned face and white forehead was startling. It was obvious that he never took it off.

Earl shook off the hands that had helped him to his feet. He ran his fingers slowly through his thinning hair and reached under a stool to retrieve his hat.

Quinn appeared out of nowhere and grabbed my arm. "What's going on here? Are you hurt?" she asked, close to my ear.

I reached up and straightened my movie star blonde wig. "That man just threatened Earl, then he pushed me!" My voice was rising to chipmunk level. I pulled my shirt down and started walking toward Nick, who was still being held back by two gym rats whose necks were nearly as thick as Nick's. "You aren't welcome here, you... you... bully."

Quinn grabbed my arm again and said, "No, Granny, you don't want to get mixed up with this." She dragged me through the crowd. We were almost to the door when Officer Baird stepped inside. He made a beeline for the fracas by the bar, while Quinn pulled me outside and away from the building.

Chapter 12

When we got home, I fell into bed. I ached all over and knew that in the morning there would be colorful bruises over a good part of my body. It seemed that I had just closed my eyes when I felt someone pulling on my arm and I tried to push them away. I rolled over on my side and put the covers over my head.

"Granny, wake up! Wake up!" My shoulder was being shaken, hard.

I opened my eyes, but the room was too dark to make out any details. Rolling over, I reached out and grabbed for whoever was shaking me.

"Quinn? What's going on?" I said groggily. "What time is it?"

Quinn jumped off the bed and turned on the lights. I looked at my bedside clock and saw that it was one in the morning. I sat up and rubbed my eyes. A pair of pants and a shirt landed on my lap. "Hurry up and get dressed," Quinn said. "Earl's barn is on fire! We've got to go help him!"

I stood up and went to the window, pulling aside the curtain. Sure enough, I could make out flames shooting into the sky. The curtain fell back into place as I swiftly turned and faced her. "Where are my shoes? Grab the phone. Call 911." I threw my clothes on over my pajamas and headed through the kitchen.

Quinn beat me to the door and held it open. We ran for the golf cart while Quinn breathlessly told me what happened. "I woke up about a half-hour ago realizing that I'd forgotten to reset the automatic sprinkler system. So, I went to the boathouse to turn it on. When I was coming home across the bridge, I saw a flickering light coming from one of the upper windows in Earl's barn. I didn't think anything of it until I pulled into our yard and saw flames coming out of that same window. I already called 911 and they are on their way."

By this time, we were coming up Earl's driveway. I could see that the entire second floor of the large red barn was on fire. I knew that Earl had animals inside. He'd told me a few days ago that one of his ewes was late in lambing.

Pulling up in front of the gate to his yard, I said, "You go wake Earl up. I'm going to go and see about getting that ewe and her lamb out of the barn." Without waiting for Quinn to say anything I went towards the barn. My tailbone injury prevented me from outright running, but I hobbled as fast as I could.

The barn was situated about 150 yards from the house next to a tall metal grain silo. It had been built about the same time as my own barn and had a similar layout. I'd been in Earl's barn many times when Chet and I had cared for his animals during his wife's illness. As I approached the barn, I looked up and saw that the flames had begun to eat away at the wall around the window and that flames were coming from all the upper-story windows. I could see the smoke, even against the inky black sky.

From inside the barn, I heard bleating. Lifting the latch on the sliding doors, I pushed with all my strength. Above me, I could hear the crackle of the flames and a loud pop followed by a bright light, and sparks rained down around me. The inside of the barn was pitch black, but not too smoky yet. My eyes began to adjust as I walked through the center walkway between the stalls.

Following the banging sound of the sheep butting her head against the door to her stall, I reached her pen about halfway down the barn. I quickly lifted the latch and swung the door open. As soon as she saw the opening, she ran towards the front door, two small lambs close behind her, bleating loudly.

The roar of the fire was getting louder above my head and I went after the sheep. I reached the doors just as Earl, Quinn, Judy, and the young man I'd seen at the park ran up to me. Judy was wearing a nightgown, Earl had a t-shirt on over his boxer shorts, and the young man was wearing designer jogging pants with no shirt. "Are there any other animals in the barn?" I asked breathlessly. "I let your ewe out. I don't know where she and the lambs went."

Earl shook his head and stared at his barn. "Go back to the house and grab the garden hoses," he said to Judy, snapping his fingers. She ran off without saying a word.

"I don't think that's going to help any," I said gently, laying a hand on his arm.

He flung my hand off and stalked away. "Not for the barn, you idiot! To keep it from spreadin'. We can hose down the surroundin' buildings."

The wailing sound of firetrucks approaching filled the night air. Quinn went to move the golf cart out of the way. I chased after Judy when I saw her struggling with a tangled hose. Designer Pants just stood there in the middle of the driveway with his arms crossed, staring at the barn. In the fleeting glance that I gave him, it almost looked like he had a smirk on his face.

We got the garden hose straightened out and Judy started spraying down everything around the barn. Quinn appeared from behind the house with another hose and hooked it up to the watering trough in one of the corrals. The noises coming from the barn were frightening. The flames were roaring, the timbers were creaking, and occasionally we could hear a crashing sound as a piece of the barn collapsed.

The heat grew more and more intense. We were forced to retreat back towards the house. The tiny streams of water from the hoses seemed to evaporate before they could do any good. Earl came up behind us and took the hose from Judy. He had a grim look on his face and sprayed the water in wide arcs on the trees and bushes around the house.

Three firetrucks came down the driveway. The reflection from their flashing lights made everything look even more surreal. Four firefighters in their yellow coats and pants piled out of the first truck and ran around to the back. They began pulling hoses out of the truck and running towards the blaze. The second truck was a water truck. Being out in the county, we don't have fire hydrants near our property and the fire department has to haul their own water. The third truck caught my attention because it was so much bigger than the other two. It was a ladder truck. One of the firemen on that truck began operating controls on the side and soon the white ladder on the top began to swing to the side and also raise up. Another man climbed up on top of the truck and extended the ladder towards the barn. I didn't notice that there was a hose hooked to the ladder until it began spraying water on the fire from above.

Earl and Quinn continued spraying water from the garden hoses on the trees and outbuildings around the barn. Judy stood next to her father with tears running down her soot-streaked face. I glanced around and couldn't see Mr. Designer Pants anywhere. Where was he? He should be by Judy's side, helping her, comforting her. I decided to go looking for him. I skirted around behind the big ladder truck and away from the barn. It felt like this nightmare had been going on for hours, but I'm sure it hadn't been all that long. The moon was obscured by some clouds, but there were plenty of stars. I made my way behind the silo on the far side of the barn. A rustling sound in the weeds made me jump. Taking a closer look, it was just the ewe and her two new lambs. They were bedded down in the shadows, barely visible.

I kept going, taking my time. Now that I was farther from the blaze, it was quieter – and darker. My left foot caught on something in the weeds and before I could catch myself, I went down on my knees. First my tailbone, now my prayer bones. What a day for an old lady. Might as well offer up a word for Earl to the Man upstairs while I'm here.

I picked myself up, brushed myself off, and found the offending stick tangled up in my shoelaces. After spending some time unsnarling it, I started to fling it back into the weeds. Something about it didn't feel right, though. It was too smooth, too regular to be an ordinary stick. I ran my fingers along its surface and discovered that the end of the stick had three long areas that felt like stiff bristles. At the other end, something had been wrapped around the object. A strong chemical smell wafted up to me.

Going back around the silo the way I had come I hurried over to the golf cart and deposited my find in the storage area at the back of the golf cart. I tried to wipe my hands on my tracksuit. It was most likely ruined anyways.

No more flames were showing from the barn and most of the firefighters were starting to put away their equipment. I saw Earl standing next to the pumper truck, talking with Tyler Flanders, the fire chief. Earl was missing his signature hat and his pale forehead seemed to glow in the dark. I walked over to them.

"It's not a total loss," Tyler was saying. "We managed to mitigate the fire before it reached the first floor. You'll have to rebuild the loft and roof, though. The fire investigator will be out pretty soon. Something doesn't feel right about this. I'm not saying it was intentionally set, but there's definitely something off. You are lucky that your neighbor called it in when they did. With as much hay as you have in there, it could have burned to the ground and taken out more property, too."

Chapter 13

Back at home, I took a quick shower to get rid of the smoke smell and eased my aching body back into bed. I sent up another prayer for the Foxman family and drifted off to sleep.

Sundays are special to me. I enjoy meeting with my congregation and worshiping together. I love listening to the weekly message and growing in spirit. What I don't love is the fake concern by parishioners just looking for gossip. Now, I'll admit, I enjoy some tasty tidbits now and then, but I know it's wrong. Especially when it is something as devastating as the fire last night. Between avoiding the millions of questions, and my sore tailbone, the church service was more than a little challenging.

After the service, Quinn and I made a hasty exit to avoid the onslaught of questions and went to the farm to make a meal for Earl and Judy and what's-his-name. I was completely surprised to see a police car sitting in front of my house when we pulled in.

As we parked the golf cart, the door of the white SUV opened and out stepped none other than Paisley Pointe's Chief of Police. Buck Ellis had a confidence about him that put everyone at ease. As he strode across the yard towards us, I took in his lanky frame and dark hair. He was not in uniform but was wearing a short-sleeved dress shirt and a pair of well-loved blue jeans.

"Good morning, ladies," Chief Ellis's big voice boomed in the still air.

"We missed you at church this morning, Buck," I said. "Come in and have a cup of coffee." I led the way through the kitchen door and directed him to have a seat. I reached for some mugs and started a fresh pot. While it brewed, I cut three slices of peach pie and put them on small plates. We kept up some small talk about the weather for a few minutes.

Clearing my throat, I said, "Now, Buck, you didn't come out here just for some pie. You're here to take statements about last night. Am I right?"

In answer, Chief Ellis reached into his left breast pocket and took out a pen and a small notebook. "Who wants to go first?"

While Quinn told Buck her story, I made myself busy, cooking up a casserole to take next door. I took ground beef and seasoned it with salt and pepper. As soon as it was nice and brown, I added some cream of chicken soup. I threw the mixture into a baking dish, sprinkled cheese over it, and covered the whole thing with frozen tater tots. I slid it into the oven and wiped my hands on a towel.

"Your turn, Granny," Buck said, taking the last bite of his pie. "What do you remember about last night?"

First, I refilled his coffee and cut him another slice of pie. Then, I gave him the rundown of events as I remembered them. "Quinn woke me up around one o'clock. I looked out the window and could see the flames from here. When we got over there, no one was around. I went to the barn to get the animals out while Quinn went to the house. Earl, Judy, and Designer Pants came out and Earl told Judy to grab the garden hose."

Buck choked on his coffee. "Designer Pants?"

"I don't know his name. Some young man who was with Judy

and Earl yesterday at the archery competition. He came out of the house with them last night. I'm guessing he's Judy's boyfriend, but we haven't been introduced. He was wearing fancy pajama bottoms and nothing else. Scrawny kid. He must have gone back inside when the fire trucks showed up. I didn't see him after that." I paused. "He looks kind of familiar, but I can't put my finger on where I've seen him before. It will come to me."

Chief Ellis stood up and stretched. "Speaking of archery. Do you know if Earl shoots arrows? Or Judy?" He stopped and grinned. "Or Designer Pants?"

Quinn and I looked at each other and we shook our heads. "Not that I know of. Why?" I asked.

"The fire investigators found an arrow in the barn that was partially burned. Could be important, probably not." He picked up his notebook and returned it to his pocket. "Thanks for the pie, Granny. And thanks for the information. I'll be in touch if I have any other questions. Great job yesterday, by the way. I enjoyed watching you compete."

I patted my Liza Minnelli wig and blushed at the praise. "Why, thank you!" I walked him to the door and closed it behind him.

The timer on the oven buzzed and I loaded the casserole and another peach pie into a cardboard box. I put everything onto the back seat of the golf cart and went to check in on the ducks. When I slid open the door, the ducks jumped to their feet. The mallard started quacking at the top of his lungs, while Peeper's tiny voice could barely be heard. I checked their dishes and saw that they had plenty of everything.

I rolled down the driveway and thought about poor Judy. Here she was, coming back home and trying to mend the relationship she had with her father, and now this tragedy happened. Knowing Earl the way I do, I'm sure he was going to try to blame this on her somehow.

The burned-out barn looked ominous in the daylight. Yellow crime scene tape had been strung around the building and several official-looking vehicles were parked nearby. One was a Paisley Pointe police car and the others had no markings on them. I could hear voices coming from inside the barn as I pulled to a stop.

I parked the golf cart right next to a gold four-door sedan in front of the white picket fence around the yard. I opened the creaky gate and walked up to the screen door. Mutt, the farm dog, hobbled out from under the lilac bush to greet me. I reached down and scratched behind his ears.

Judy appeared in the doorway.

"Hi there, Judy." I studied the girl. She was tall and thin. She had piled her dishwater blonde hair on top of her head in a dancer's bun. She still held some of the qualities of the little girl I remembered before her mother died, like her meek demeanor and her fluid grace. "I just came to check on you and your dad. I brought you some food. How are you holding up?"

Judy opened the screen door and stepped outside. She took the box and said, "Thank you." She turned and placed it on the floor inside the house. Then she came back outside, carefully closing the door behind her. "I'm doing... alright, I guess. It's good of you to stop by." She glanced nervously over her shoulder. "How about we sit in the shade and visit?" She gestured to a pair of ornate cast iron bistro chairs placed artfully next to the lilac bushes in the shade of the old cottonwood tree.

"I'm so glad you've come home," I said, searching for a safe topic of conversation. "You are so grown up now." Coming right out and talking about last night felt too abrupt.

Judy crossed her ankles and picked at some dog hair on her tan capris. "Yeah, I had to do a lot of growing up after Mom died. But apparently, I haven't done enough. Dad still treats me like a little girl." There was a hardness around her mouth and eyes that spoke of deep hurt.

"Speaking of Earl, where is your dad?"

Judy shrugged. "I don't know. We had a big fight last night after he got home from that party at the restaurant. He took off and must have come home after I went to bed. Then, after the firemen left, he took off again." She looked about ready to cry.

I looked around the yard, trying to give her a chance to compose herself. "Oh, look! Your dad still has that giant ceramic sheep that you won at the county fair. You were eleven or so, I think." I laughed at the memory.

The corners of Judy's mouth went up a tiny bit. "It needs to be repainted." The sheep was about two feet tall and three feet long. From a distance, it looked like a real sheep.

I noticed that Judy kept watching the back door of the house. Then, when Judy reached up to tuck a strand of hair behind her ear, a sparkle caught my eye. "Judy Foxman, is that an engagement ring on your finger?" I reached out and caught the girl's hand in my own. The ring had a single, princess-cut diamond set in platinum. It was petite, just like Judy.

Judy blushed and nodded. "That's why I came back home. I wanted Dad to meet Ivan and give us his blessing. I hoped that we could work things out and start fresh, you know."

I felt a huge lump form in my throat. Tears pricked my eyes and I turned away, pretending to admire the lilac blooms.

Judy took a ragged breath. "Dad has always been disappointed in me. Nothing I ever did made him proud, you know? I finally have some success in my life and come home to try and mend the relationship and he rips everything out from under me." She wiped the tears from her cheeks with her fist.

She was just getting started. "You want to know what the fight was about yesterday? I'll tell you. I'm not engaged, Granny, I'm married. That's what I wanted to tell Dad. Ivan got here yesterday. We went with Dad to the archery thing, but it wasn't the right time to talk about personal stuff. Then, we waited for him to get home from that party. He came home in a sour mood. We should have waited until this morning to talk."

I pictured Earl being taken down by Nick Zeppa and the slug-fest that ensued. I could imagine just what that sour mood looked like.

"Dad doesn't like Ivan. They yelled a bunch." Judy hugged herself and started rocking back and forth. "Then Dad said he was taking me out of his Will. That's right. Me. His only daughter. Out of the Will. Then he started swearing and saying that he'd rather see the farm destroyed than let us have it. He said he was going to take me out of his Will."

Judy covered her mouth with her hand. "When Dad stormed out of the house, Ivan went after him. Ivan came back a while later and said he couldn't find him." She glanced toward the house again.

"Granny, I'm afraid. I'm afraid that either Dad did this to prove a point, or..." she lowered her voice, "Ivan did it to get back at him for rejecting us. You should have seen how mad he was. It scared me."

Chapter 14

I drove home slowly, thinking about what Judy had said. Could her fiancé, erm, husband, have been the one to set the fire? Or would Earl get so mad as to burn down his own property out of spite? By the time I pulled up by my own back door, my head was spinning. Nothing made sense. I also considered the fact that Nick had threatened Earl last night. And what about that comment that Corrie had made last week about lighting a match? It seemed that there were lots of people who would love to see Earl ruined. Maybe even Judy herself.

Shaking my head to clear out all the conflicting information, I decided that a visit to the resident patient was in order. Being around the animals always helped me calm down. I opened the barn door and was greeted by a chorus of quacks. Dragging an old kitchen chair over next to the pen, I sat down and watched the ducks. I could feel the tension leaving my neck as the ducks waddled around, walking through their water pan, nibbling on their food.

Every once in a while, Harvey would turn his head and sort of nibble on the dressings that bound his injured wing to his body. "Hang in there, buddy. You have an appointment with Doc soon to get that nasty thing off. I'm so sorry that you got hit by an arrow—"

I froze. The arrow. Smooth shaft, bristly end. Jumping up, I ran toward the house. I could hear Harvey making a ruckus behind me. "Sorry guys. Got to check something out really quick."

When I got to the back of the golf cart, I reached down and pulled out the stick that had tripped me last night. Except that it wasn't a stick. It was an arrow. A black arrow with neon yellow fletching. Wrapped around the tip was a rag, held there with a black zip tie. Part of the rag looked burnt. A strong chemical smell came from it. I carefully placed it back in the cargo hold and closed my eyes.

The next morning, I was up bright and early. Not because I wanted to, but because I couldn't sleep. My brain just wouldn't shut off and I kept going over what had happened, trying to make sense of it. After checking the clock umpteen times, I decided that it was time to go to town. I had people to talk to. Facts to check.

It was my habit to check on Harvey before I left the farm, so I went out to the barn. But when I slid the door open, no quacks greeted me. I quickly crossed the floor to the temporary pen. No Peeper, no Harvey. I checked the perimeter and sure enough, those pesky animals had created their own back door, right next to the haystack. I searched the barn but came up empty. They had been there when I did the chores that morning, so they couldn't have gone too far.

I raced outside and checked the corrals, the chicken coop, and the pigpen. Nothing. Wags and Brock followed me around. "You haven't seen two runaway ducks, have you?" All I got in return was a slobbery kiss or two. I tugged on my wig as I thought about where those rascals could be. I'd decided to go with silver curls today, I was certainly feeling my age with all the bumps and bruises I had. No Hollywood glamour wig for me.

Just then, I heard a very faint peep. It was coming from the golf cart, of all places! I walked over to where it was plugged in by the back door and sure enough, those two rascals were sitting on the floorboards, as pretty as you please. They looked up at me and I swear Peeper was smiling.

"How did you two get here?" I said.

"Quack!" came the mallard's answer. He wiggled his tail feathers. Peeper looked at me with big, liquid eyes.

I went into the laundry room and grabbed the cat carrier. Soon, I had both ducks back inside the pen in the barn. And I put hay bales all around it, just to make sure they stayed put.

At the Harp Street vet clinic, Eryn was not at the front desk, so I slipped through the door to the examination rooms. I wandered from room to room until I found Doc Worthington in the storage room counting boxes. "Hi, Doc," I said, knocking on the door frame. "Didn't want to scare you."

"What's up?" Doc put down his clipboard. His black hair was standing on end like he'd been pulling on it. His cheeks sported stubble. There was a yellow stain on his white lab coat, just below the breast pocket. I noticed that there were deep circles under his eyes, too.

"I just have a quick question for you," I said, picking up some kind of silver implement and turning it over in my hand.

Doc took the tool from me and set it on a stainless steel tray. "Ask me anything, Granny. What can I help you with?"

"You wouldn't happen to still have that arrow you removed from the mallard's wing, would you?"

Doc moved to the other side of the room and rummaged in a cabinet. "You mean this arrow?" He held up a large plastic bag. Inside were the two pieces of the arrow that he had removed last week. "I always save what I can from animal cruelty cases. I know you said it was an accident during archery practice, but you never know if it was done maliciously. Anyone who injures or tortures an animal needs to be prosecuted. Did you figure out who did it?"

I grasped the bag and studied the arrow. There was no doubt about it. With the black shaft and the bright yellow fletching, this arrow looked very much like the one I'd found out at Earl's farm.

I shook my head. "No, I still don't know, but it might have a connection to something else that happened." I paused.

Doc groaned. "Did they shoot another duck? What is happening in our community?" He ran a hand through his hair.

Patting Doc's arm, I said quietly, "Not a duck. This time they tried to burn down Earl's barn. I found another arrow out at his farm. Looks like they were trying to use it to cause a fire."

"You've got to be kidding!" Doc stumbled backward, sitting down hard on a stool next to his microscope equipment. "I know that he's a little rough around the edges, but sheesh! Who would want to do that?" Doc rubbed his stubbly chin with a fist. "He called me on Saturday morning, asking for advice. He thinks Judy's man is up to something suspicious. You don't think he did this, do you? Were there animals in the barn?" His face, under the peeling, sunburned skin, looked a little green.

"You OK, Doc? Do you need me to get you something? A drink of water?" I picked up some papers that were lying on the counter and started fanning him. It was like he couldn't hear me.

Eryn came running into the room. "Hurry, Doc!" she said, out of breath. "A dog's been hit by a car!"

Without a word, not even a goodbye, Doc took off down the hall to the reception area. I stood there for a few minutes, thinking about what Doc had said about trouble with Judy's boyfriend. I was still holding the bag with the broken arrow. I turned it over in my hands. From the little I knew about archery, it seemed that the more expert shooters had all brought their own arrows that were unique to them. If these two arrows belonged to the same person, it should be fairly easy to track down.

I took some pictures of the arrow with my phone, put it back in the cupboard, and headed out the door.

CORRIE WAGNER, DIRECTOR, the nameplate said. I knocked on the door.

"It's open."

The Paisley Pointe Recreation Center had recently been renovated and this was the first time I had been in the director's office. The walls were painted a pale green. A counter top with a single-cup coffee maker ran down one wall. A large window overlooking the municipal golf course graced the wall opposite the door. An ornate walnut desk stood in front of the window. Shelves holding photos and target shooting trophies made up the third wall.

Corrie sat at the desk, surrounded by paperwork. Her stout, muscular physique looked out of place in the light gray business suit she was wearing. She had put on makeup and her hair was styled in soft curls that lay on her shoulders. She was almost unrecognizable. I was used to seeing her wearing polo shirts and tennis skirts with her dark hair pulled up in a ponytail.

"You sure do clean up nice," I said, approaching the desk. I stopped in front of Corrie and looked at what she was working on. Some of the papers were covered with columns of numbers.

Corrie sighed and looked up, fiddling with a pen. "What can I help you with, Granny. I'm kind of in the middle of something."

She reached into a candy dish and pulled out a mint. The cellophane wrapper made a crinkling noise as she opened it.

Scrunching my eyebrows together, I said, "I'm sorry to bother you. I did knock, you know. I can come by another time when you aren't so busy."

Putting the pen down on the desk, Corrie stood up and walked to the window. "You're here now. Just spit it out."

"I'll make it quick. I just wanted to ask you a question about the arrows some of the archers used this weekend."

"So, what's your question?" Corrie had turned to face me, arms crossed. She crunched down on her candy.

"Um... well... I guess my question is, are they all different?" It wasn't the question I really wanted to ask, but Corrie wasn't exactly being chatty. Not that she ever was.

Stacking some papers together and clipping them, Corrie said, "Yes, and no. You know that many of the competitors used arrows provided by the rec center because they don't have their own. Some of the more elite shooters brought their own. When competitors are using the same arrows, we have to spread them out so they aren't on the same target. There are only so many color combinations out there unless you have custom arrows made. But those are expensive." She laughed. "Way out of your price range."

"Did anyone this weekend have custom arrows?" I wondered.

Corrie nodded. "There were a few people who did. Both of the finalists were using arrows that were custom ordered through the rec center. I actually helped design the ones that Lucy used to win." She smiled proudly.

"Design? I didn't know you could design arrows. Lucy's were very bright and easy to see from far away. Good job."

"It's all in the details," Corrie said, sitting back down.

I asked, "How many did she have made?"

"Only six. Like I said, they are expensive. Look, I'd love to chat more, but I'm due at a town council meeting in a little while. You can show yourself out." With that, she picked up her pen and started to write on a yellow notepad.

I turned on my heel and left the room. I'd never been dismissed like that before. It made me feel like second class. Not a point in Corrie's favor.

An idea came to me and I headed for the front counter. A young woman with purple hair and a nose ring sat there, flipping through a magazine. I waited for her to look up. When she didn't, I cleared my throat. "Excuse me."

"What?" the girl asked, not looking up. She flipped a page.

"I'd like to check out some archery equipment, please," I was using my best old person voice.

A clipboard landed in front of me. "Fill this out."

OK, then. I took a pen from the cup and wrote my name on the form and checked the boxes for what I needed. Handing it back, I asked, "Would it be possible for me to pick the arrows out myself? I find that some colors work better for me than others. I'm a little bit color blind." I smiled at the top of the girl's purple head.

Slapping her magazine down on the desk, the girl stood up. "Fine. Follow me." She picked up my form and walked down the hall behind the desk.

The equipment room could be described as controlled chaos. There were large trashcans lining one wall filled with hockey sticks, pool noodles, and arrows. A rack behind them held a line of bows. Shelves along another wall held clear plastic containers filled with smaller equipment.

Purple Hair pointed at the rack of bows. "Pick what you want."

She leaned against the doorway and studied her long, black fingernails.

I walked over to the can full of arrows. There was a multitude of colors of both shafts and fletching. None of them were black with the neon yellow feathers that I'd seen in Harvey's wing or at Earl's farm.

"Are these the arrows that were used at the competition this past weekend?" I asked. I ran my fingers along the fletching of a blue arrow. I looked over to the doorway, but my companion had disappeared. I walked over to the door and glanced up and down the hallway. I could hear the receptionist talking to someone on the phone. No one else appeared to be around, so I went back into the equipment room and started looking on the shelves and behind the equipment. I just had this feeling that if there were two arrows alike, there had to be more. Didn't they always come in groups of six? And if someone from the rec center was responsible for what happened, they might try to hide the rest of the arrows.

I dug around in metal baskets holding football pads, in lockers for jerseys. A dozen or so gold bags stored in one corner sort of tipped over when I tripped on a strap and fell into them. And added another layer of bruises to my already battered body. After wallowing around like a turtle on its back, I managed to make it to my feet and set the bags upright again.

After thoroughly scouring the messy room, I limped toward the door. Well, that was a dead end. I reached for the light switch and turned to leave when something caught my eye. A slender black box was tucked under a shelf on the floor right next to the open door. It definitely looked out of place.

Just then, Purple Hair returned. "Can't find what you need?" she asked, snapping her gum.

"I... um... changed my mind. I'll come back another time. Thanks for the help." Scooting around her, I bolted for the front door and fresh air.

Chapter 15

I climbed slowly into the golf cart and rubbed my sore legs. If I kept this up, I'll be black and blue all over. I decided that some sustenance was in order. I pointed the cart towards Main Street and the café. At this time of day, the place would most likely be empty.

I hobbled inside and got a cup of coffee from Nora. "You aren't moving too good, Granny. Are you OK?"

I smiled sweetly and said, "Bad knees. Growing old stinks." I took a seat by the window that overlooked the park. I sat and sipped and watched the town. In the park, some kids were playing frisbee with their dog. A young woman jogged past wearing earbuds. Cars drove slowly down the brick-paved street.

I saw all of this but didn't really pay attention. My mind was focused on trying to figure out a connection between the arrows. Maybe there wasn't one. But something in my gut told me that there was. I needed to get a look at the arrow that was found in the barn.

"Thanks for the coffee, Nora. I'll see you tomorrow." All that sitting had stiffened me up again and it took a while to get my muscles warmed up to where I could walk without limping.

Parking directly in front of the glass doors at the Harp Street Vet Clinic, I breezed through the door and past the reception desk. I had almost made it to the inner door when Eryn stopped me.

"Hello, again, Granny. Back so soon? Is there something I can help you with?" She smiled but tilted her head towards the waiting area. She has really good people skills. I need to remember to tell Doc that.

I shook my head and opened the door, ignoring the subtle hint. "No, that's alright, honey. Doc asked me to come back and pick up some ointment for that wild mallard. It looks like its wound might be getting infected." I sent up a quick prayer apologizing for the lie.

"He never told me about it," Eryn frowned, standing up from her rolling chair. "Let me—"

I pulled the door open and shut it behind me. I hobbled quickly down the hall to the storage room. I let myself in and looked around. I felt a bit guilty about lying to the sweet girl. Making a beeline for the cabinet where Doc had put the arrow, I didn't see the young tech coming from between the rows of shelving until it was too late.

We both crashed to the ground, taking with us a stainless-steel tray filled with instruments and dressings. The young man in the lab coat straightened his glasses and jumped to his feet. "I am so sorry!" he said. "I didn't see you there. Are you hurt?"

"Nothing but my pride, sonny," I said, reaching my hand out to him. "Help me up, please." After some awkward positioning, I managed to get my feet back under me and stand up to my full, intimidating four feet eleven inches. I pulled my lavender shirt down over my elastic-waisted warm-up pants and said, "Well, that was exciting. Let me help you clean up this mess so that you can get back to work."

The door burst open and Doc rushed in. "Is everything OK in

here?" He paused and did a double-take. "Granny? What are you doing back here?" He pushed his glasses back up his nose. It didn't seem possible, but his hair was even messier than it had been earlier.

"Nothing but a little fender bender," I said, rubbing my backside and looking at the tech. He nodded sheepishly and looked down at the tray in his hands. "I thought maybe I left my reading glasses in here." I made a pretense of looking around the pristine room. Doc was a bit of a neat freak and insisted that even the supplies be organized and lined up in exact rows. "Nope. Not here. Sorry for the crash." I walked around Doc and out the door before he could say anything.

I saw an open door across the hall and scooted inside. It was an empty examination room with vinyl chairs and a stainless-steel table. It was an exact duplicate of the one we'd used when I brought Harvey in. I pulled the door closed until there was just a sliver to look through. I watched the hall and waited until Doc and the young man came out, carrying supplies to a room down the hall.

Once the coast was clear, I crept on tip-toes back into the storeroom and went to the cabinets. I pulled out the bag containing the broken arrow and tucked it into the back of my sweatpants. I pulled my shirt down over it. *Good thing I wore my stretchy pants today.* I looked up at the ceiling and whispered, "I'm just borrowing it. I promise to return it soon."

I sauntered back to the front and waved to Eryn as I left. As I pulled the golf cart onto the street, I glanced over my shoulder, feeling guilty for what I was doing. Not enough to undo it, but guilty just the same.

Back at the farm, I grabbed one of my fresh pies from the refrigerator, covered it with plastic wrap, and put it into a large cloth market bag. I removed Harvey's broken arrow from its hiding place and looked it over carefully. I didn't want to remove it from the plastic, so I stood next to the window to get the best lighting. The arrow was just a wooden dowel that had been painted black. The feathers were not only glued to the shaft but also partially recessed into slits in the wood. They were shaped in a way that the end closest to the nock where you placed the bowstring was longer than the end closest to the arrow tip, giving the arrow a streamlined look.

Satisfied that I had memorized the details, I added the arrow to the market bag. I took a moment in the bathroom to check myself in the mirror. I straightened my wig and fluffed the silvery curls. It was looking a little worse for the wear. I needed to take it to Priscilla's for a wash and set.

After applying a coat of Mystic Rose lipstick, I grabbed my bag and walked outside. It was time to wrangle some information out of the police chief.

Chapter 16

Two sets of shaking tail feathers greeted me when I got to the golf cart. Those ducks were almost certainly smiling at me. Shaking my head, I decided to let them stay. Maybe a little fresh air would be good for them. I climbed onto the seat and we set off to town. I kept a close eye on the birds, thinking that they might try to jump out, but they settled down next to each other and looked very contented.

I passed the café and the flower shop, turning left on the next street heading away from the park. The town hall was located a block from Main Street and directly across from the Pointe of No Return. Locals bragged that the restaurant was home to the best hamburger and micro-brewery in the county.

The small police department occupied offices in the town hall next to the mayor's office and the county clerk. Parking the golf cart, I admonished the two ducks. "Don't you go anywhere. I'll be right back." Harvey and Peeper looked at me solemnly and there was a small peep from Peeper. Satisfied that they would listen, I headed up the sidewalk. I know, I know, how can you trust a duck?

I let myself in and marched across the wide expanse of tile that made up the entry hall, up to the bulletproof glass that separated the common room from the sergeant's desk. Rapping on the window, I startled an officer who had been staring intently at a computer screen.

He sat up and said, "What can I do for you?" His bushy eyebrows hovered over deep-set gray eyes. There was a mustard stain on his dark blue uniform and I pointed to it.

"First, you can tell Buck Ellis that Irma Appleton is here to see him, and then you can go and clean that off your shirt." I crossed my arms and waited.

The officer glanced down at a clipboard and said, "Do you have an appointment? I don't see your name on the list. Chief Ellis isn't taking calls or visitors at the moment. He's up to his neck in alligators over the arson. Can I help you with something?" He brushed a hand self-consciously over the mustard.

"I understand he's busy, son," I said, softening my tone a little, "but I have information about the fire that he will want to see. Just go tell him I'm here."

Standing up, the officer started for the hallway behind the desk. He glanced back at me, and I made shooing gestures at him with my hands. He disappeared through the first door on the right and I waited, watching the clock.

Hearing voices echoing across the tile foyer behind me, I glanced around. Walking in from the entrance on the opposite side was a young, thin woman in a flowered dress with a full skirt and a man wearing a dark blue suit with skinny trousers and wingtip shoes. I recognized Judy Foxman. She had certainly grown out of her tomboy phase into a beautiful, graceful woman. In spite of the fights and hard feelings, I knew it had broken Earl's heart when she left Paisley Pointe. The young man with her was the one I'd seen at the archery competition, and again the night of the fire – Ivan, her husband. Judy was hanging onto his arm, looking up at him as though the sun would set on his command. That feeling came back to me, I *knew* I had seen him somewhere before.

She doesn't look like someone who just suffered a catastrophic fire, I thought to myself. Spotting a large terracotta planter sporting a rubber plant, I sprinted across the floor and wriggled myself behind it.

I peeked around the planter. Judy and her man hadn't seen me. As they came closer, I heard Judy say, "Are you sure this is the right thing to do, Ivan?" Now that he was closer, I thought he looked like he belonged in one of those late-night commercials that advertise get-rich-quick schemes. His dark hair was oiled straight back. His thin jaw was as smooth as a baby's bottom. His shoulders were narrow and he looked like a good stiff wind could knock him over.

Ivan turned on a 1,000-watt smile and patted her arm. "Of course, Dumpling. Your father will thank us for this. What better legacy to leave his little girl than to make her the wealthiest woman in the county?" Even his voice was thin. It sounded more like a little boy's voice than a man's.

The couple turned and headed towards the county clerk's office. In his free hand, Ivan was carrying a large black case with a company logo embossed on its glossy surface. My eyes narrowed. That logo! Now I knew who he was. He was the snake who had come by my farm last spring, trying to buy my place to develop into expensive condos. My farm fronts the Paisley River, making it prime real estate. Earl's farm borders the river, too.

I was so intent on watching them that it took me a minute to register that someone was clearing their throat right next to me. I looked up to see Police Chief Buck Ellis staring down at me. "Lose something, Granny?" There was a smirk on his face as he watched me extricate myself from my hiding place.

"Maybe I did," I retorted, feeling my face flush. My hair caught on a part of the rubber plant and it pulled my wig over my ear. I yanked on it and marched past him with as much dignity as I could muster.

Chief Ellis followed me to the door. Out of the corner of my eye, I could see that he was pressing his lips together. He'd better not laugh. He swiped his security card and when it beeped, held the door open for me. This wasn't my first visit to his office, and I'm sure it wasn't going to be the last. We had known each other for years. In fact, he is family. Buck had married my niece, Vivian.

Turning the corner into Buck's office, I swept past the imitation leather couch and scuffed coffee table. I plopped myself down on a chair covered in hunter-green microfiber facing Buck's desk. I put my canvas market bag in my lap and waited for Buck to ease himself into the swiveling office chair with the lumbar support. I helped Vivian pick it out as a Christmas gift last year.

"I'm kinda busy here, Granny," Buck began. "I heard from the desk sergeant that you had some information about the barn fire at Earl's place." He rested his elbows on the arms of his chair and tented his fingers.

I made him wait. I felt it was only fair since he'd made me wait. I looked around the office, taking in the American flag just behind his right shoulder. A Marine Corps flag was on the left side of the room, along with another of those giant planters. Pictures on the wall showed Buck with Vivian and their two children at Hoover Dam, at the ocean, and in front of a podium. The last picture was taken when he became the chief of police for Paisley Pointe. I remembered how proud I had been that day.

Buck was a good man and a great leader.

When I deemed that I had made him wait long enough, I said, “I might.” I leaned back and shrugged my shoulders. “It depends.”

Buck shifted in his seat. “On what?” he asked. His eyes darted to the file folder sitting in the middle of his desk. “You know you can’t withhold information about a crime, Granny.”

I had been watching him closely, like a poker player looking for tells. “On what’s in that folder right there. The word around town is that it was an accident. That there was some faulty wiring or something.”

Buck nodded his head. “That’s what we thought, too.”

“What if I have evidence that it might not have been an accident?” I asked. “I heard the fire chief say there was something not quite right about it.”

“I’m listening.” Buck leaned forward and crossed his arms over the folder in front of him.

I leaned forward, too. “You first.”

Buck shook his head. “Nope. I am running an investigation here. This isn’t a two-way street, you know. If you have evidence that I need to know about, it’s your obligation as an upstanding citizen to share that with me.”

I looked down at the bag in my lap. My shoulders sagged. I gave a loud sigh and said, “Alright.” I reached inside and pulled out the plastic bag from the vet clinic. Buck’s eyebrows went up.

“What is that?” he asked.

I laid the bag on the desk and pushed it closer to him. “Doc Worthington pulled this arrow out of a mallard in the park on Monday. The duck survived. I’m taking care of him. As a matter of fact, he hitched a ride with me to come here.” I chuckled. “We named him Harvey. He and my white duck, Peeper, are pretty inseparable now."

Buck had picked up the bag and was turning it over in his hands. "What does this have to do with the fire in Earl's barn?"

"By itself, nothing," I said, reaching back into my bag. "But I also found this by the silo on the backside of Earl's barn the night of the fire." Feeling just a little smug, I pulled out my trump card and laid another clear plastic bag on the desk. "These are designer arrows, Buck. They look *exactly* like the ones that Lucy Cantana used to win the archery competition. How did her arrow get on Earl's farm? And why is she shooting ducks?"

Buck's eyes were as big as saucers for a split second. Then he carefully rearranged his expression to look interested, but not too interested. Instead of picking up the arrow, he looked at his black tactical military watch. "Granny, I really appreciate you bringing all of this in. I need to talk to some people now. I'll have Vivian give you a call. We'll have you and Quinn over from dinner sometime soon, OK?" He stood up and walked towards the door.

I didn't move from my seat. "Oh! I also brought you a pie," I said. I reached into the bag and brought it out. I placed the tote on the floor under my chair and put the pie on the desk next to the file folder. "It's a new recipe. Quinn really liked it and couldn't believe the main ingredient. I wanted to see if you could guess it. I'll go grab a fork out of the break room." I jumped up and was out of the room before Buck could react.

When I returned a minute later, he was back behind his desk inspecting the second arrow. I peeled the plastic wrap back and cut a wedge of pie. Sliding it onto a paper plate I'd found, I handed it to Buck. "Take a bite. I know you'll love it." I clasped my hands and hovered next to him, watching. Buck had always had a weakness for my pies.

He dug the fork through the crumbles sprinkled on top and into the smooth, creamy, yellowish-green filling. “Is it key lime?” he asked, holding up the fork to study it.

I shook my head and smiled.

He put it in his mouth and chewed. “Wow!” he said. “That’s really good. It’s kind of like a custard. I can’t place the flavor, though.” He took another healthy-sized bite. “I want to say egg cream, but there’s no cinnamon.” He looked at the ceiling for a moment.

I beamed. Nothing made me happier than when people were enjoying my baking. I was also tickled that Buck was forgetting that he was trying to get me to leave.

“I give up. What kind of delicious concoction is this?” He scraped up the last bits of pie with the edge of his fork. “I’m going to have to hide this from my staff so I can take it home to Vivian. She’s going to flip over it.”

“If you really want to know, it’s a zucchini pie,” I said triumphantly.

Buck’s jaw dropped and he looked at his plate. “There’s no way that you made that dessert out of a sweaty squash,” he said. “Unbelievable!”

I placed the plastic wrap over the remaining pie. “Well, that’s one way to get stubborn men to eat their vegetables. I guess I’d best be going. You should put that pie in the refrigerator so it stays firm.” I watched Buck pick it up and then followed him to the door. I turned left toward the exit and he went to the right toward the break room at the far end of the hall.

I walked the few steps to the front counter and stopped. Lightly smacking my forehead, I said to the desk sergeant, “Silly me! I left my bag in the chief’s office.” Laughing at myself, I turned around and walked back. Shutting the door softly, I stole to the desk and opened the file folder. On the top page was a close-up photo of an arrow lying on charred wood. A black arrow with neon yellow fletching. The next ones were a series of photos from different angles all around the arrow. In some of them, you could see the wall and window of the upper story of the barn with the silo in the background.

Chapter 17

I hustled out of the town hall. The information I had just learned confirmed my suspicions. My mind was going a million miles an hour. Sure, Earl wasn't easy to get along with. He was a know-it-all, self-righteous person. But who would get so mad at him that they would want to ruin his property and risk the lives of innocent animals?

I was almost to the golf cart before I saw that a crowd had gathered around it. "What's going on here?" I asked, pushing my way through to the vehicle.

Lucy Cantana was standing next to the driver's side. "You have ducks in your golf cart," she said, pointing. Peeper and Harvey were no longer on the floorboards. They had decided to settle on the passenger seat. People in the crowd chuckled.

Someone called out, "Can they drive that thing?"

I climbed in and released the brake. "Not until they get their permits," I said as if it was an everyday occurrence to drive around with animals in your golf cart. The crowd parted when I started backing up, and I took off.

As I drove, I looked at the ducks next to me. They were both sitting on the seat, facing forward, looking through the windshield. Harvey let out a loud quack. Peeper nibbled on my arm. I smiled and ran a hand down her smooth back.

Peeper had come to my farm the way most of my animals had. They were rejects or castoffs from people who didn't think things through. People who made an impulse decision based on emotions and then didn't have the resources or skill to care for the animals for the long term. Baby animals don't stay babies forever.

Besides the duck, I had also inherited a donkey, a goat, and a lot of chickens. I loved every one of them, too. I loved their personalities. Being a farmer's wife, dealing with livestock had come with the territory. Now that my husband was gone, I was extra glad for their companionship. I was glad that Peeper had taken Harvey under her wing, quite literally, because being a wild animal, I wasn't too sure about how he would fit in on the farm.

Peeper shifted positions and something shiny caught my eye. Harvey was sitting on something metal. I pulled the cart over to the side of the road and picked Peeper up. She squeaked in protest. Harvey let out a loud quack and stood to his feet, raising up his one good wing. He was ready to come to Peeper's defense. When he stood up, I got a good look at what he'd been sitting on. It was a key chain. I picked it up. Turning it over in my hand, I saw that the charm on the chain was a little mug with the letter 'L' on it.

"Now just where did the two of you get this little item?" I scolded the ducks. "You won't be allowed to come with me on trips to town if you start taking things that don't belong to you!" I put the keys into the tote bag and pulled back out onto the road.

Quinn's work truck was parked next to the back door. I drove the golf cart to the barn and put the ducks back into their pen. I'd have to ask Quinn to help me change Harvey's dressing after supper. I was glad to have Quinn around the farm, but I was worried about her. Ever since her art critic ex-boyfriend had ruined her burgeoning art career in New York, Quinn had not been herself. She was shy and introverted and it was taking some time to build up her confidence.

I found my granddaughter behind the barn filling the water tank in the donkey's pen. I reached for a pitchfork, went back into the barn, and stabbed a flake of alfalfa off of an open bale at the base of the haystack. I came back to the corral. Throwing the hay over the fence, I asked, "How was your day?"

"Busy," Quinn said, making swirls in the water with the hose. "I've been trying to get all the annuals planted in containers around the businesses in town. Between that, repairing damage to the park, and catching up on the maintenance at the ball field, I'm bushed." Quinn looked at me out of the corner of her eye. "How about you? Are you doing OK? How's your knee? That accident at Foxman's place has me a little rattled. I want to go through our barn and check out the wiring to make sure we don't end up in the same boat."

I leaned the pitchfork against the fence, watching the donkey munch on its dinner. "What if I told you that it wasn't faulty wiring that caused that fire?" I said. "What if I told you that someone did it deliberately?"

Quinn was still holding the hose. She turned quickly, spraying water all over me. She closed the nozzle, swallowing hard. "I'm so sorry. Did you say it was done on purpose?" The last word came out as a squeak.

Water from my wig was dripping down into my eyes, so I pulled the bedraggled thing off my head and smoothed my natural hair down. Looking at the ruined hairpiece woefully, I said, "That's right. I managed to peek at some pictures from the fire investigator. Whoever did this used a fire arrow to light the place up."

"An arrow?" Quinn seemed incapable of making her own words. She sounded like a parrot. "But I thought that old barn had some frayed electrical wires." She shook her head. "I'm confused."

"I'm guessing that whoever did this thought that the arrow would burn with the building and people would just assume that it was an accident."

Wrinkling her forehead, Quinn asked, "Who would do something like that? Why would they want to burn his barn down? I know he's cantankerous, but he didn't deserve this." Her eyes got suddenly wide. "What if they come here next and try to burn ours down?"

I squeezed some water out of my wig. "I agree. He didn't deserve this. Someone either really hates him, or he did something to them to make them really mad. Or there's a pyromaniac on the loose. I intend to get to the bottom of this. I have an idea of where to start looking." I reached into my pocket and pulled out the key chain that Harvey had absconded and waved it in front of Quinn. "I think we should go have dinner in town."

Quinn groaned. "Not again. Lucy's going to be furious."

"It's her own fault. If she would just put the whole thing inside her pocket like a normal person instead of dangling it halfway out, she wouldn't keep dropping them," I said.

After making sure that the ducks were safely tucked in for the night, we shut the barn doors. Then we headed for town.

The Pointe of No Return was a large restaurant and was a very popular place for folks to gather. It was getting dark when Quinn and I walked up to the building. The closest parking space we could find was a block and a half away. Even the parking lot at the town hall had been full.

The outside of the building was made of rough-hewn timbers and locally sourced river rock. Strings of lights made the place warm and inviting. The tables on the patio to the side of the entrance were packed with people. We heaved the heavy wooden door open and made our way to the hostess stand. While we waited to be seated, we looked around and chatted.

Warm, honey-colored wood seemed to be the theme. The lights were recessed into the ceiling. The long, highly polished bar was fronted by short logs that had been arranged in a pattern. Some lay longways, some had been chopped so that their round ends were displayed. Behind the bar, a team of five bartenders was working. There were rustic-looking barrels on stands behind them. Two large copper brew tanks made up the centerpiece.

"Appleton? Table for two?" I heard behind me. When I turned around, there was Purple Hair Girl! She looked completely bored and didn't seem to recognize me. Of course, I had changed my wig after the dousing with the hose. I was now sporting a blonde pageboy cut.

Our table gave us a great view of the action behind the bar. As we ate our burgers, I watched Lucy work.

Lucy was wearing a white tank top with the restaurant's logo on it. Over that she had on a black men's dress shirt with the sleeves rolled up and the tails tied in a knot under her large bosom. Her dark hair was pulled up in a messy bun. Her winged eyeliner was dark and heavy. She was very efficient and greeted everyone at the bar by name. She didn't smile much, but was friendly and stopped to talk to people.

Quinn reached over and squeezed my arm. "Don't look now, but that horrible guy who fought with Earl after the archery competition just walked in!" Her eyes went big and she motioned with her head.

I turned in my chair. The big, muscle-bound man strode across the room, not even waiting for the hostess. He was wearing a pair of black ripped jeans that looked painted onto his bulky thighs. His light gray ribbed shirt was stretched to capacity and open at the neck. An iron cross pendant lay on his hairless chest in the opening. His short dark hair was full of product and stood straight up all over his head in little points. His beard was trimmed close and accentuated his strong jawline.

He walked right past our table without looking at us. My eyes watered from the wave of aftershave he left behind. Walking up to the bar, he called for Lucy in a loud voice. We watched as Lucy and the man talked over the bar. It was too noisy in the restaurant for us to hear what was said, but the expression on Lucy's face went from neutral to confused to angry in the space of a minute.

The waitress came over to the table just then and stood between me and the show. "Is there anything else I can get you?" she asked sweetly.

I was straining to see around her. "I think we're fine. Thank you," I said absentmindedly.

The waitress turned to leave.

I said, "Wait! Can you tell me about the man at the bar? The one talking to the bartender." I pointed.

The waitress put her hand over her heart and sighed. "Oh, you don't know. That's Nick Zeppa. He's a famous bodybuilder. He wins competitions all over the state. Isn't he amazing?" She flounced off to help another table. She moved just in time for me to see Nick pick up a glass from the bar and splash its contents into Lucy's face.

Quinn gasped. Lucy picked up the soda gun and sprayed water

on Nick. With a roar, Nick lunged for Lucy. Lucy roared back and punched Nick square in the face. Just then, two guys who were obviously security rushed up and got on either side of Nick. Lucy walked to the other end of the bar and toweled off her face. The bouncers managed to turn Nick around and escort him to the door.

Lucy watched him leave with hooded eyes. Her mouth was set in a straight line. I sure would have loved to know what she was thinking.

We finished our meal and headed home. One of my favorite true crime shows was on and we sat together in the living room to watch. The clock on the mantle in the comfortably shabby room chimed the hour. Quinn stood up, stretched, and yawned.

"I'm going to turn in. I have a big day tomorrow. I want to finish the planters and the filter in the sprinkler pump at the lake needs to be cleaned. That's always a messy headache to deal with." She kissed the top of my head and went to her room.

I also got up and headed to the kitchen for a glass of water. I stood looking out the window toward Earl's farm. I could just see the lights on in his house through the trees. I wondered how Judy had gotten involved with that man, Ivan.

When I reached my room, I started to change out of my clothes. When my sweat pants hit the floor, the keys Harvey had stolen fell out of the pocket. I picked them up and said, "Well, well, well. Look what we have here. I must be getting soft in the head." I put my clothes back on and tiptoed out of the house.

Back at the Pointe of No Return, I found that the dinner crowd had cleared out. There were only a few people scattered around the dining room. I was worried that maybe Lucy's shift was over and she had already left. The wait staff had begun their nightly cleaning ritual, stacking chairs, sweeping, and mopping. Purple

Girl was nowhere in sight. Then I saw Lucy polishing glassware at the bar and headed over.

Smiling, I climbed up onto one of the bar stools directly in front of Lucy. "What can I get for you?" Lucy asked.

"Oh, I think I'll just have a cup of coffee if you don't mind," I said. I took one of the stir sticks from the container on the bar and fiddled with it. Lucy filled a thick white mug and set it in front of me with a bowl filled with little cups of creamer.

"That was quite the altercation you had earlier," I said, pouring sugar and creamer into the cup. I stirred it thoroughly and took a sip. "I can't believe the nerve of that guy." I took another sip and watched Lucy over the rim. "What was he wanting, anyway?"

Lucy shrugged and picked up another glass to dry. "That was my little brother, Nico. He's a hothead."

"Your little brother? I didn't know you had family here in Paisley Pointe."

"His girlfriend kicked him out, so he's living with me for a while. He thinks he's some big shot since he won a couple of trophies. Get this. He changed his name to Nick Zeppa, thinking it makes him sound more professional. I think it makes him sound like an idiot."

"What did he want from you? He seemed pretty steamed."

Lucy put the glass down. "Him and every other bum around here keeps asking for a cut of my winnings. He has some big business deal or something. I've got plans for that money. He can go get his own."

Lucy was fairly new in town, only having been there a few years. I knew that she lived in a small basement apartment on the edge of town. She spent a lot of time at the rec center and joined several of the town's sports teams. When you live far away from the big cities, local sporting events had a big draw for entertainment, both for participants and spectators.

"What *are* you planning to do with the money, if you don't mind my asking?"

Lucy looked up and down the bar before answering. "See those giant vats?" She used her thumb to point over her shoulder at the big copper pots. "That's the owner's idea of a micro brew. It's OK, I guess, but I've been working on my own recipes."

I was impressed. "That sounds like a wonderful idea. Are you going to open up your own place?"

"That was the plan," Lucy said. She had a sour look on her face. "Then that stupid nosy Foxman started spreading rumors about me. Now no one will give me the time of day. I tried to get a loan from the bank, but they turned me down flat. I know it's because of him."

"Rumors? What kind of rumors?" I took another sip of coffee. Definitely not as good as Nora's coffee.

"He was in here one day talking about leasing his land since he's retired now. I told him I was interested in growing some hops. He'd never heard of them and thought that was an illegal substance and started telling everyone I was a drug dealer."

I had indeed heard all about those rumors. Earl had done a good job of making sure everyone in town knew. I might have even believed it for a while. I didn't tell Lucy that, though.

"I'm lucky to still have my job," Lucy said. "Maybe now that he has something of his own to worry about, instead of ruining my life, my dreams can get back on track."

Knowing how hard it was to change people's minds once they were made up, I doubted it. I decided to change the subject. "I got to watch you in the final round at the archery competition on Saturday. I have to tell you, I was mighty impressed with your technique. I just can't seem to get the knack of it."

Lucy grinned, the first real one I had seen from her all night. "I love archery. I've been doing it since I was a child. I love the feel of the bow, the breath control, and the sound of the arrow striking the target. It takes a lot of concentration. It helps me take my mind off my problems." She leaned in and put the towel on her shoulder. "I especially love beating the guys. They always seem to think that since I'm a girl, I can't be good at it. The look on their faces when I out shoot them makes me all warm inside."

As Lucy refilled my coffee, I said, "I couldn't help but notice how pretty your arrows were. I've never seen that bright neon yellow on an arrow before." I know, I know. All these little white lies are going to catch up to me.

"I had those custom made," Lucy said. "My old arrows were pretty beat up because I practice so much. I've been working extra hard on my long-distance shooting lately. Plus, this was a chance to win some big cash, so I went all in. Good arrows can make or break you."

"Wow, I wish I could have seen them up close. I've only used the ones the rec center supplies. Pretty low quality, if you ask me. I'm sure they are nothing compared to yours."

Lucy had started wiping down the bar with her towel. "I've got them in my car right now if you'd like to see them." She motioned for one of the other bartenders to take over.

"Speaking of cars," I said, "I believe these belong to you." I held out the key chain. "I found them in my golf cart." Not technically a lie.

"That blasted duck took them again?" Lucy exclaimed. She snatched them out of my hand and led the way out the back door to the employee parking lot.

Lucy's small green economy car was parked next to the street light. It didn't fit the image I had for her at all. I had pictured her driving a truck or a sporty SUV. Not a beat-up, faded old car with mismatched wheels. Lucy went to the trunk and unlocked it. She reached inside and pulled out a long, thin black box. Closing the trunk lid, she set the box down gently and opened it.

I felt a tingling in my fingers. I had studied the arrow from the park and the one I had tripped over. I had looked very closely at the photos of the arrow in Earl's barn. I could already picture what I would see in the box.

Nestled into the foam inside were six black arrows, alternating directions. I counted them carefully. Six. The box was full. There were no empty slots for more.

Picking up one of the arrows, Lucy handed it to me, and I held it up to the light. "These are magnificent!" I gushed. I turned the arrow every which way and hefted the weight. "Is this all of them?" I asked. There just had to be more.

Lucy laughed. "As expensive as these are, yes." She took the arrow from me. "Look at how true they are," she said. She grasped it in both hands and bent it. The arrow sprang back to its original shape. "These babies are made of carbon fiber. They are just flexible enough to bend around the bow but stiff enough to always go back to true."

As Lucy was conducting her demonstration, a small detail caught my eye. "What's that?" I asked, pointing to the area just below the nock.

"I had my initials embossed on each one after I got them," Lucy said. "I didn't want there to be any questions about whose arrows these were. You're looking at arrows that cost me over a grand."

I only half heard what Lucy was saying. I was trying to picture the arrows from the barn fire in my mind's eye. I couldn't remember the detail around the nock area. The arrow from Harvey's wing had been made of wood, but what about the others?

"Thanks for showing me," I said. "These are amazing. I learned a lot this evening. Good luck with your micro brew." I patted Lucy on the shoulder and turned to walk around the building to my golf cart.

Lucy had turned to put the arrows back in the trunk. "If I ever get my prize money," she muttered.

I stopped. "What was that?"

"Oh, nothing. There was apparently a mix-up at the bank. I haven't received my prize money yet."

Chapter 18

In the morning, I started the day with my usual chores. When I opened the barn doors to get feed, I was greeted by loud quacks and little tiny peeps. The two ducks were standing inside the door, wagging their tail feathers.

"How are you two getting out of your pen?" I asked. I inspected the chicken wire and couldn't find anything. Then I noticed a small space next to the haystack where it looked like they had burrowed out again.

It had been a week since Harvey's unfortunate injury. I could tell by the way that he was acting that it was time to remove the bandage. As soon as the chores were completed, I went to the house to grab the cat crate I'd used to bring him home. When I came back out, both ducks were sitting on the front seat, waiting for me. "I guess we don't need this," I said, laughing. I put the crate on the back seat along with my market bag containing the waterlogged wig. I planned to go to the beauty salon after taking Harvey to the vet. Better to combine trips so as to not waste time.

It was a beautiful morning. The sun was shining, the air was still a little bit cool. The fruit trees were all in flower and filled the air with their sweet scent. I enjoyed the drive, as much from the company as the scenery. The ducks kept up a quiet conversation as they peered through the windshield. I smiled at them and wondered what they were saying to each other.

When we reached the Harp Street Clinic, I wondered how to get Harvey inside the building. Would he walk in with me, or would I have to use the crate after all? My question was answered when the two ducks hopped down and followed me to the door.

In the waiting room, Eryn laughed at the visitors. "What's this?" she asked.

"I think Harvey is ready to have his bandages removed," I said. As if in agreement, Harvey let out a particularly loud quack and nibbled at the white wrappings.

"I'll go get Doc," Eryn said. "He's not going to believe this."

Soon, she returned with Doc Worthington in tow. He was wearing a crisp white lab coat and it looked like he had at least made an attempt to tame his unruly black hair. "Well, what do you know," he said, hands on his hips. "It's not every day that my feathered patients walk themselves into the clinic. Hello, Peeper." He bent down to give the big white duck a scritch under her bill. He had made friends with Peeper on his many visits to the farm. "Will they follow you to the exam room?" he asked.

"I guess we're about to find out," I said. I held up the carrier. "We can always use this if we need to." I started towards the hall door. The ducks formed a line behind me and waddled in my wake. I kept glancing over my shoulder as the merry parade made its way down the hallway. Heads appeared in doorways to watch our progress.

Doc removed the bandages and examined the wound. Harvey sat quietly on the table and didn't make a sound. Peeper, on the other hand, kept trying to fly up onto the table. After several failed attempts, I picked her up and plopped her next to Harvey. She immediately settled down and nuzzled her friend's neck.

"Just as I suspected," Doc said with a frown. "He'll never be able to fly again. But it looks like he might have found his forever family." He smiled at the two ducks and looked at me. "You *are* planning to keep him, aren't you?"

"I wouldn't have it any other way, and neither would Peeper," I said, running my hand over Harvey's glistening back. "It is strange, though, how much he behaves like a pet. He must be pretty young and impressionable."

We said our goodbyes and waddled our way out of the building, followed by the staff, all with their cell phones out taking videos. Harvey's left wing drooped a little, brushing the ground.

When I took my wig to True Colors, the ducks came, too. I tried to get them to stay in the golf cart, but they refused to be left behind. The bell over the door jingled. Priscilla came out of the back room, took one look at the ducks, and laughed. "You know you live in a small town when your customers bring their pet ducks to the salon. I guess it's no different than someone bringing their Pomeranian."

I grinned. "I'm glad you understand. I didn't plan on having them with me, but here we are." I held up the ruined wig. "I was hoping that you could do something with this."

Priscilla took the wig to the washing station and poured some shampoo into her hand. "Have a seat. This will take a little while. Tell me about your, erm, pets."

I sat down in the waiting area. The armchairs were deep and comfortable. The ducks disappeared underneath the coffee table. I told her Harvey's story and how Doc had removed the arrow.

"Arrow, you say?" Priscilla said, clucking her tongue. She shook her blonde curls and I noticed she had dyed the ends a vibrant pink that matched the stylish frames of her glasses. "You don't think someone shot the duck deliberately, do you? I'd hate to think someone did that for sport."

I watched her rinse the wig. The shop was bright and sunny. The three styling stations were empty at the moment, but it was early. It wouldn't be long before this place was full of gossiping women.

Priscilla said, "Did you hear about what happened to poor Earl Foxman? His barn burned to the ground. The buzz around town is that it wasn't an accident. Some people are saying that he caught Lucy Cantana cheating last weekend and she lit the barn on fire in retaliation. I'm not saying she did, but she sure wasn't a very gracious winner. She's been making a stink about her money all week. Betsy Rollins told me yesterday that Lucy was screaming at the bank manager."

I raised my eyebrows at this but didn't say anything. The town's gossip mill was as bad as a game of telephone. I watched Priscilla expertly roll the wig into an absorbent towel and squeeze it. Then she placed the wig on a stand and started to section the hair. She wrapped the sections around giant rollers.

Outside the window, there was a loud rumble, almost like thunder. We both turned to look. A large black truck idled at the stop sign, then roared away, rattling the windows. Priscilla shook her head. "Every day, that blasted man comes by here driving like a hotshot. I don't know what Corrie sees in him."

"Who?" I asked. I had a pretty good idea what the answer was, but Priscilla was the switchboard operator of the town gossip line and I wanted to see if she had any new information.

"Nick Zeppa. He's new in town. Corrie Wagner thinks he's the best thing since sliced bread. She claims they are dating, but I haven't seen them out together. He's some kind of athlete. All I know is that he is disturbing the peace with that big truck. You know what they say about men with big trucks." She waggled her eyebrows. Setting the wig stand under a hairdryer, she turned the heat to low. A gentle hum came from the machine.

Priscilla came and sat in a chair next to me. "This will probably be the only chance I get to sit down today." She propped her feet up on the coffee table and leaned back. We sat in companionable silence for a few minutes.

"I hear that Judy Foxman brought herself a boyfriend home to meet her daddy. Did you know that?" Priscilla asked. "He's some hoity-toity land developer from back east somewhere. Nora told me that she overheard Mayor Springer say that he is going get Earl to let him have land to build some high-end houses along the river."

I thought about what I'd seen at the town hall. I started seeing red. No wonder there had been an argument between Earl and Judy's man. Earl was a proud farmer. He might be retired, but he still loved his land and would never want to see it dug up and built into a suburban neighborhood. Something didn't smell right about the whole situation.

The timer on the hairdryer dinged. Priscilla got up and lifted the wig stand onto the station counter. She removed the rollers and brushed out the wig. "There," she said, "good as new."

The ducks piled back into the golf cart as if they'd been doing it all their lives. I released the brake and just as I pressed the accelerator, I noticed Harvey holding something in his beak. It was a bobby pin from the salon. Sighing, I pressed the brake and said, "You are going to be trouble, aren't you?"

I wrangled the pin from the duck's bill and took it back inside, placing it on the nearest counter. I could hear Priscilla in the back on the phone. "Slow down, Corrie. I don't understand. You say that Lucy's dating who? Nick? Aren't you dating him?" Water started running and I couldn't hear any more.

Chapter 19

I decided that it was time that I went back to visit the Foxman farm. Earl and Judy might need some help with the clean-up. If the investigation was wrapped up, that is. I hadn't visited sooner so that I wouldn't be in the way.

Stopping off at the house, I went to the kitchen. I couldn't just show up empty-handed. So, I decided to bake a pie. What kind of pie says I'm sorry your barn burned down? A traditional raisin pie, I decided. If it's good enough for an Amish funeral, it would work in this situation. I grabbed a boxful of raisins and placed them in a sauce pot, along with cinnamon and sugar. When the filling was boiling, I filled the pie shell I had whipped up and covered it with more pie dough.

When the brown flaky pie came out of the oven, I set it on a rack to cool while I changed clothes. I didn't know how Earl's dog would react to the ducks, so I made sure they were securely locked in the barn before I left.

As I drove down the road, I could see Earl's old yellow truck on the side of the road. He was leaning over the ditch, setting the pipes that brought water from the irrigation ditch, through the fields, to his crops. I guess he wasn't nearly as retired as he claimed to be.

When I drove into the yard at the Foxman farm, I noticed that the yellow caution tape was still stretched around the barn. The burned rafters stood out in stark contrast to the blue cloudless sky. There was only one car parked in front of the white picket fence that surrounded the yard. It was a large, gold-colored four-door sedan. It sat next to the large lilac bushes that framed the gate. The bushes were in full bloom. I let myself into the yard and approached the screened-in back porch. Out in the country, almost no one used the front door.

Beautiful rose bushes filled the flowerbeds under the windows. I knew that soon there would be yellow, red, and pink roses everywhere. I knocked on the screen door and called, "Judy? Are you there? It's Granny Appleton from next door." I stood back and waited. Earl's old farm dog came and sniffed at my leg. His muzzle was completely white and I could see that the poor thing had cataracts in both eyes. I reached down and patted him on the head.

Stepping back up to the door, I knocked again. And waited. Looking through the screen, I noticed that the door to the kitchen was open. I called, "Yoo-hoo! Judy! It's Granny. I've brought you a pie." I opened the screen door. It squeaked loudly. Stepping across the wooden porch floor, I peeked into the kitchen. There were dishes piled in the sink and the trash can was overflowing.

Somewhere inside a door slammed. I stepped inside and put the pie next to a messy pile of papers on the Formica table in the middle of the room. I walked across the sticky floor to the doorway leading into the dining room. The house was eerily quiet.

Outside, someone started a car. I went back into the kitchen and looked out the back window just in time to see the gold car spraying gravel as it left the yard. There was only one person in the vehicle. And it wasn't Judy.

My hands started to tingle. "Judy? Are you in here?" A soft mewling sound came from behind one of the closed doors off the kitchen. I threw the door open. It was the master bedroom. Earl's bedroom. The covers were in a messy pile on the bed and clothes were draped over a chair in the corner. A gray and white cat shot out from under the bed and ran through the house.

I stepped to the other side of the kitchen and opened another door. A smaller bedroom, decorated in pink. This one had to be Judy's old room. It looked like a time capsule with teenage heartthrob posters on the wall and costume jewelry draped around the mirror over the dresser. But no Judy. I called out again. A small thump sounded on the other side of the wall. I ran from the bedroom, through the kitchen, and into the dining room. Another closed door.

Feeling a sense of panic, I opened the door and saw a third bedroom. This one was in disarray. The blankets and sheets were twisted and half off the bed. The dresser drawers were all open and clothes were scattered all over the floor. The closet door was half off the hinges. I scanned the room but didn't see anyone. The window was open and the curtains swayed in the slight breeze.

Suddenly, another sound came from the far side of the bed. Stepping carefully across the messy floor, I rounded the end of the bed. There, on the floor, slumped against the wall, was Judy. Half of her hair had fallen out of her usual bun and become tangled. Her eyes were vacant and there was drool trickling from one side of her mouth. Relieved to see that her chest was moving, I knelt beside her and called her name.

"Judy? It's me, Granny. What happened? Can you talk?" I reached for the girl's thin wrist and could feel how thready and fast her pulse was. I reached into my pocket and pulled out my cell phone to dial 911. On the bedside table, I spotted a bottle of sleeping pills.

While we waited for the ambulance to arrive, I managed to get Judy up off the floor and to the couch in the living room. I brought her a glass of water, but Judy sat, unresponsive, almost like she was in a trance. I sat next to her and kept an eye on her breathing and pulse. I tried to get her to talk, but it was like sitting with a ghost. She sure was pale enough to be one.

Paramedics arrived, followed by Earl. They bundled Judy onto a gurney. After explaining to Earl what had happened, he turned and followed the ambulance to the hospital in his truck. Standing alone in the silent house, I remembered the cat. I went in search of the poor thing. I didn't want it to be locked up in the house all alone. Plus, it gave me a chance to look around.

I'm not snooping, I told myself, *I'm helping a neighbor.*

The house was a little messy, but nothing like that bedroom. The strange thing was, the only clothes I could see were Judy's. There was nothing belonging to her husband, Ivan. It was as if Judy had made that story up. If I hadn't seen them together at the park and the town hall, or seen him drive away in the gold car, he might have just been a figment of Judy's imagination.

In the kitchen, I filled a container with water and set it on the floor. I hadn't been able to catch the skittish kitty. I searched in the cabinets and finally found some cat food. I poured some into a dish and set it next to the water.

The papers on the table caught my eye. I knew that reading someone's mail was wrong, but this was lying out in plain view. I saw the decorative edge of another document peeking out of the pile. A marriage license. So, it was true. Judy really had gotten married. The name of her husband was Ivan Kruptek.

I recognized the town logo on another document. Sliding the top pages over with my fingernail, I saw that it was a land-use permit application. With Judy's name as the applicant.

Chapter 20

After locking up the house, I returned home. I felt the need to bake some more pies. I did my best thinking while rolling out pie dough and mixing ingredients. There was just something about it that calmed my brain and helped me focus. And boy, did I have a lot to think about.

I put on my favorite apron and pulled out the flour. A chocolate cream pie was just the ticket. When I opened the container, there was only about a cup of flour left. Sighing, I took off my apron and grabbed my market bag.

I had left the ducks in the barn so they couldn't come with me. Driving down the dirt road, I thought about poor Judy. What had happened? Had she had a reaction to the medication sitting on the bedside table? Had she taken too much? Was it an accident? There seemed to be too many of those happening lately.

I wasn't paying attention to the road and when I got to the bridge, the front tire of the golf cart found the edge of a loose board. The golf cart bounced hard, almost sending me flying. I managed to get control of it just before crashing into the guard rail. I sat there for a minute, waiting for my heartbeat to return to normal. Then I drove into town at a more sedate speed.

There was a large, chain-type grocery store on the west side of town, but I preferred the small shop that was located close to the vet clinic on Harp Street. I wanted to do my part in keeping the local, family-owned businesses alive.

Manuel's Market had a small produce section up front, three rows of shelves in the middle, and a meat counter in the back. Manuel himself was at the checkout counter bagging a customer's groceries when I pushed through the door. "Howdy, Ms. Appleton. What can I do you for?"

"Hi, Manuel. Just had to restock my pie ingredients." I grabbed a basket and made a beeline for the baking aisle. I knew exactly where to find what I needed. The flour was located on the bottom shelf near the back of the store. I set my basket on the floor and reached for a five-pound bag. As I did, I noticed a small slip of paper jammed halfway under the long industrial shelving.

I slid it out and unfolded it. On one side, I saw that it had been torn from one of the fliers advertising the archery competition. On the other side was a note, scrawled in blue ink. The handwriting was scratchy. It said, "I know what you did to that barn. Meet me by the boathouse tonight at 11 or I go to the cops."

I knew that Manuel was meticulous with his cleaning. Every night he swept and mopped the store himself. I had been the last customer of the night on more than one occasion and knew his routine. This note had to have been dropped sometime today. Looking around, there was no one in sight. In fact, now that the other customer had left, I was the only shopper in the whole store. I folded the note up again and tucked it inside my wig. Patting my hair, I stood up and walked to the front.

I didn't see Manuel, so I browsed through the produce. Finding some blueberries, I added them to my basket. A blueberry pie would be fun to make, in addition to the chocolate. I could hear

Manuel back at the meat counter. He was running the grinder, making hamburger meat. I walked to the back and stood there, watching him for a minute.

There was a small bell on the top of the meat case. I tapped it once. Manuel shut off the machine and went to the sink. After washing his hands, he came up to the glass cabinet. "Did you see something you like, Ms. Appleton? I have some great jalapeno bacon here." His large black mustache obscured his mouth. His blue eyes crinkled in the corners.

"You know I don't like spicy foods, Manuel. How about two of those pork chops instead. I'll make some scalloped potatoes to go with them for supper tonight." As I talked, I was thinking about how to use food to sweet talk Quinn into helping me spy on someone.

As Manuel wrapped my purchases in white butcher paper, I asked, "How's business? Are you keeping busy?"

Manuel wrote on the outside of the package with his grease pencil. He nodded and said, "Oh, yes. The business has been good. We are keeping busy. I'm thinking about stocking some of those protein powders. You know, like Mr. Atlas uses on TV? That bodybuilder man came in and asked for some. Corrie Wagner says that it would sell like hotcakes."

We walked up to the front and Manuel rang up my purchases. "Good luck with your protein powder," I said as I left.

That evening Quinn and I sat at the kitchen table, savoring the last bites of the chocolate pie. Over dinner, I told Quinn about finding Judy and getting her to the hospital. We agreed that we should go and visit her in the morning.

"That guy she married sounds like a snake," Quinn said. "I feel sorry for her. I hope she'll be OK. I guess I should be glad that I got away from Ricardo when I did. I probably would have ended up just like her."

I looked across the table at my granddaughter and was so grateful to have her living here with me. When Quinn's relationship had fallen apart, I had been her safety net. We had always had a special bond. But I was working on a plan to get her back in the dating game. She could take as long as she needed to heal from her broken heart, but it couldn't hurt to help, right?

Putting that thought on the back burner, I stood up and took my plate to the sink. I returned to my seat and asked, "Do you have any plans for the evening?" I brushed some imaginary crumbs from the table.

Quinn put down her fork and looked at me. "Not really. Why? Do you want to put together a puzzle or something?"

"I have something a little more... active... in mind," I said with a grin.

Chapter 21

At ten o'clock we were sitting in the front seat of Quinn's work truck, dressed in black shirts and pants. The night sky was clear and full of twinkling stars. In the background, a chorus of frogs was singing in harmony with the crickets.

"Let me get this straight. You found a note on the floor of a grocery store that told you that someone knows what happened to Earl's barn and they are going to blackmail the person tonight. And you want to eavesdrop on the conversation. And then what?" Quinn ticked off the points on her fingers. "Sounds a little flimsy to me."

I nodded. "That's right." I pulled the note from under the dark wig I had chosen for this mission. "See, eleven o'clock tonight. We'll hide in the boathouse and listen to what happens."

"And then what? Confront the person? The *arsonist*. Why don't you just take the note to Chief Ellis or Officer Baird? Let them handle the situation," Quinn the Sensible said.

"Do you really think that they would take this note seriously? You, yourself, are doubting its credibility. If *we* do it, and it turns out to be nothing, then the police haven't wasted their time on a useless clue. If it turns out to be true, then we can take the evidence to the chief and they can be the heroes. I think it is a win-win proposition." I was excited. This was going to be fun.

"I'm not planning on confronting anyone. Just see who shows up and learn what they know. We should get into place early before anyone shows up." I opened the door and stepped out. Quinn followed, slamming her door.

"Shh!" I admonished. We had parked on one of the side streets that branched off of the one that curved around the park. "We don't want to draw any attention, remember?"

"Sorry," Quinn said, in a stage whisper. "This is my first time spying. I haven't the foggiest idea how to do things."

We made our way down the street. I crouched over. Quinn walked upright. When we reached the boathouse, we stood against the wall. Quinn pulled her keys out of her pocket and unlocked the door. We slipped inside and I turned on the tiny flashlight I had brought. There was some rolled-up garden hose hanging on a peg. Maintenance equipment filled most of the space. There was a workbench with some tools against the wall closest to the door. A couple of lawn chairs were sitting against the wall opposite the door.

We sat down and I turned off the light. The room was black, with only a little bit of light shining through tiny pinholes in the walls from the streetlights. At first, I couldn't hear anything but Quinn's and my own breathing, but after a while, I started noticing other sounds. The water lapping at the shore. The crickets and frogs around the lake. An occasional car driving by. Then, I heard a new noise – footsteps. Someone was walking on the gravel path around the edge of the lake! I reached out and gripped Quinn's arm.

The footsteps got closer. The door handle started jiggling and we heard a key in the lock. Quinn grabbed my arm and we hurried to the far side of the shed, feeling along the wall as we went. I couldn't remember everything I'd seen in the few seconds I'd had the light on, so I followed close behind Quinn. A large gang mower was parked in front of the garage-style door at the far end of the shed. I banged my shin on the mower deck and bit my lip to keep from gasping. Another bruise to add to my collection. We crouched behind the mower just as the door swung open.

The silhouette showed that the person was tall and had broad shoulders. I couldn't see much else. I couldn't even tell if it was a man or a woman. My heart was pounding in my chest. The adrenaline was flowing. This was it! Then the door clicked shut.

A flashlight beam cut the darkness as the person swept it across the room. I peered through the gap between the seat back and bottom. Quinn put her hand on my head and forced me to duck down lower. The light paused on the two lawn chairs, then slowly made its way towards our hiding place. It traced the shape of the mower, then continued around to the other wall. Just before the person clicked the light off, the flashlight glinted off of something metal in the person's gloved hand. I heard the creak of a lawn chair as the person settled in. A cellophane wrapper was being opened. Crunching noises.

I could feel a Charlie horse forming in my right calf. As my muscles tightened, the pain radiated down to my foot. My toes started cramping and curling in my walking shoes. I bit down on my lip again to keep from crying out. My eyes watered from the pain. I slowly reached one hand down and tried to massage my leg.

After what seemed like an hour of shallow breathing, we heard the person in the chair shift around, like they heard something. Then I heard it, too. Quinn stiffened beside me. Another set of footsteps on the gravel outside. The lawn chair creaked as the person stood up and walked to the door. There was a faint knock.

A police siren blipped and a blinding light showed through the cracks in the walls. "What are you doing there?" came a voice over a loudspeaker. Outside, the person took off running. I was at once happy and disappointed. It was good to know that the Paisley Pointe Police Force was doing nightly patrols, but now I wouldn't find out who was supposed to meet up tonight.

The person at the door didn't move for several minutes. It was as if they had been turned to stone. Which meant that Quinn, me, and Charlie horse were stuck where we were, too. I've got to remember to put bananas on my shopping list. Especially if this spying business keeps up.

Finally, the door opened and the mystery person slipped out. Quinn immediately stood up and stretched. I slowly unfolded my creaking joints and limped around, trying to get rid of the pain. We waited around for a while, then cracked open the door. Not seeing anything out of the ordinary, we locked the door behind us and made our way back to the truck.

"First thing tomorrow, that lock gets changed," Quinn said between gritted teeth.

Over breakfast the next morning, Quinn and I discussed our little adventure.

"Who do you think that was?" Quinn asked around a forkful of fluffy eggs. Our chickens were producing eggs at a phenomenal rate. If we didn't eat eggs just about every day, we'd be overrun with them.

I adjusted my black pageboy wig and shrugged my shoulders. "I'm not sure. The only thing I saw was that they were big. But maybe that's just because I was scared."

Quinn bit into her toast. "The thing that bothers me most is that they had a key to the boathouse. I thought I had the only one. Last week, I found the boathouse door unlocked and thought that I had forgotten to lock it. Now I'm wondering if that person has been in there before. Why would they want a key to an old shed? The only things in there are tools, the pump controls for the sprinklers, and that gang mower."

I thought for a minute and sipped my coffee. "Maybe we ought to look inside in the daylight. There's got to be a reason."

"Maybe after we go visit Judy in the hospital," Quinn said.

When we left the house, Peeper and Harvey were waiting for us in the golf cart. "Alright, you two. You can't visit the hospital with us. Everybody out." I tried to shoo them, but they wouldn't budge. I picked up Peeper and put him on the ground. When I turned to get Harvey, Peeper jumped back in.

Quinn laughed and said, "Good luck, Granny. Those ducks look determined to take a ride. Maybe you should take them to the lake and leave them for a swim. I think that's the only way you'll get them out of that cart." She jumped into her work truck and took off.

I stood, hands on hips, and looked at my passengers. "So, you want to go to town, do you?" In response, I got a quack and a peep. "Alrighty then. To town you shall go."

The boathouse looked a lot less spooky in the daylight. I pulled up next to it and parked. Harvey jumped down, quacking up a storm, and made for the water. His left wing dragged on the ground, but he didn't let it slow him down. Peeper followed in his wake. I watched to make sure that Harvey didn't have trouble in the water. This was his first time going swimming since the accident. I smiled as I watched him go tail-up in the shallows.

Leaving the ducks to their fun, I walked back to the golf cart.

On my way to the hospital, I stopped in at Divina's flower shop for a bouquet. Knocking on Judy's door, I pushed it open. Judy lay in the bed with an IV in her arm. Her skin looked even paler against the white sheets and there were dark circles under her eyes. Even so, she looked beautiful. I could see a lot of her mother's features in her. In the recliner by the window, Earl sat with his head back and his eyes closed. When Judy saw me, she clicked off the TV.

Rushing to the side of the bed, I bent to hug the young girl. "Oh, Judy." A lump in my throat prevented me from saying any more. When I stood back up, I noticed that there were tears in Judy's eyes. I put the flowers down on the rolling table next to the bed and took Judy's cold smooth hand between my warm ones.

"Thank you for coming to see me," Judy said softly. She looked towards the door. "Did Ivan come with you?"

I said, "No. I haven't seen him. He hasn't come to the hospital?" Then I asked, "What happened yesterday? Do you remember?" The door clicked open behind me and Judy looked over my shoulder, her face lighting up.

"Hi, Quinn," Judy said, visibly disappointed. The smile left her face and she looked down at her hands.

Earl cleared his throat and stood up, stretching. "It's gettin' a mite crowded in here. Think I'll go stretch my legs and give you gals a chance to talk. Maybe find me a coffee machine."

Judy pinched the bridge of her nose. "Dad's been here with me the whole time. He only left for a little while to take care of the animals at the farm. He doesn't know where Ivan is, either."

A nurse in blue scrubs came into the room with her computer to take Judy's vitals. She placed the blood pressure cuff on Judy's arm and started the machine. "You must be Judy's grandmother," she said. "It's so nice of you to visit. What beautiful flowers you brought!"

Judy started to protest, but I said, "Yes, I am. I came to take my precious granddaughter home."

"Oh, her chart says she is to stay here for another two days, at least, for observation," the nurse said, frowning. "The ER had to pump out her stomach yesterday. She could have died from all that medication." She picked up Judy's wrist and looked at her watch. After taking her temperature and marking all the numbers down, the nurse left.

"Granny, I didn't take a bunch of medicine, I swear! I don't know what that nurse is talking about." Judy's eyes were wide and she shook her head. "Ivan and I were fighting about the farm, and I had a headache. I get terrible migraines sometimes. He gave me a glass of milk to help me sleep and... Oh! You don't think he... The staff here thinks I tried to..."

I smoothed Judy's hair and shook my head. "Sounds like you need to talk to Chief Ellis." I pulled out my cell phone and dialed the number from memory.

When the chief arrived, Quinn and I left them to talk in private, and to go find Earl. He was going to want to be there for Judy. That dirty, good-for-nothing Ivan was trying to swindle the Foxman family out of their land. For once, his distrust for people was well-founded.

Chapter 22

I drove towards Paisley Park slowly, thinking. Maybe it was Ivan who had set the fire. It all fit. He had shown up a year ago, trying to buy property on the river. I hadn't been interested in selling and neither had Earl. Ivan found out about Earl's daughter. He tracked her down and seduced her, convincing her to marry him. He got Judy on his side, promising her buckets of money when they developed the property. She wants to please her man and keep the peace. The only problem was that Ivan didn't count on Earl being such a stubborn old cuss. When Earl wouldn't agree to help his new son-in-law out with property, he tried to burn down the farm so that Earl couldn't use it. And Judy probably sided with her dad. She didn't want the farm to turn into a housing development. Ivan got angry and decided that he needed Judy out of the way. Maybe he was planning to get Earl out of the way, too. Since Ivan and Judy were married, he would inherit everything and could put his plan into motion.

At least that was the way I saw it. But I had no way to prove it. Yet. I headed back to the lake to pick up the ducks. I didn't want to leave them for too long, since Harvey was vulnerable to predators. As I watched Harvey paddle toward me, following Peeper, I started to have second thoughts. Sure, Ivan had a motive, but the arrow. Ivan didn't have access to arrows, did he? Was there someone else who wanted to ruin Earl? Cause him harm?

I thought back to snippets of conversation I'd heard around town. Earl wasn't a very well-liked man. He was opinionated and found fault with everyone, including me. When I'd brought him a pie at Christmastime, he'd complained that the filling wasn't creamy enough. It was a little thing, true, but it had gotten under my skin, nonetheless.

Something was going on between Earl and Corrie, too. That morning at the coffee shop, when he'd mumbled under his breath. What was it he'd said? Something about Corrie's evaluation. What was that about? She knew that Earl had been against the archery competition from the start. He wasn't happy having all the extra people in town. Could that have upset someone enough to start that fire? Had he tried to manipulate the contest to make it fail? Lucy still hadn't gotten her prize money. Did Earl have something to do with that?

With the ducks on board, I decided it was time to find some answers. We headed for the recreation center. The parking lot was full, so I drove around to the back lot by the golf course. I spotted Corrie on the driving range.

I had forgotten about the ducks until someone yelled, "Hey, look! It's Mother Goose!" I looked behind me and saw that my two friends were trailing me across the grass. Ignoring the laughs, I continued across the greens and stopped behind Corrie. The sun was warm on my shoulders and there was a slight breeze. She was concentrating on her grip and didn't hear us coming.

Corrie was in mid-swing when Harvey decided it was a good time to let her know we were there. He let out an extra loud barrage of quacks. She let go of her golf club and it flew downrange. "What are you doing here, Granny? And where did these blasted ducks come from? Get them out of here! I hate ducks. They are filthy animals."

I just stood there. "Beautiful day, isn't it?"

"It was until you came along," she muttered. "What do you want?" She eyed the ducks warily.

"I was in the neighborhood and thought I'd drop by for a chat."

"I'm not in the mood. I came out here to relax for a few minutes," Corrie snapped.

Innocently, I asked, "Relax? Is everything OK? You have seemed a little tense lately."

Corrie ignored me and took another golf club from her bag. "I have half a mind to use this on your pets." She set a ball on a tee, lined up, and swung her hardest. The ball flew into the air and sailed to the flag posting 150 yards.

"Nice drive," I said.

Pulling another ball out of the basket, Corrie said, "Thanks." She hit another one, but Harvey's quack was timed perfectly with her swing, causing her to miss the ball completely. "Are you going to stand there all day? Don't you have something else to do?"

"Actually, no," I said. "It's so nice out here, the ducks and I are going to stay all day."

Corrie stooped and grabbed her water bottle. Twisting off the cap, she said, "Fine. What do you want to chat about?" Peeper waddled closer to her and started nibbling on her shoelaces. She backed up and put her golf bag between her and the duck.

"I was hoping you'd tell me why Earl was so mad at you last week."

Corrie paused with the bottle halfway to her lips. She creased her eyebrows for a second. "Oh, that. It was nothing. Just a little misunderstanding. Earl is on the board of directors for the rec center and thought I was trying to take money from one of the programs to pay out the purse for the archery competition. The entry fees alone covered that cost. It was all straightened out."

"Was it? I heard that Lucy still hasn't received her $25,000 for winning."

"What!?" Corrie gripped the bottle so hard that her knuckles turned white. "That lying piece of —-. She's trying to spread rumors about me. She knows that the money has to be issued by the town as a certified check. And it wasn't $25,000. That prize money was split between the top three competitors."

"That's not what the posters said." Behind me came a small sound. Peeper was agreeing with me. Harvey was busy playing with something he had found in the grass. It was a golf tee.

Corrie picked up her golf bag and the bucket of balls. "You have to read the fine print. Now, if you'll excuse me, I have a spin class to supervise." She stalked off toward the pro shop.

I turned to the ducks. "Oh, the lies. That woman is hiding something." Harvey tried to quack around his treasure. He and Peeper followed me as I crossed the asphalt towards my cart. As we approached the building, the back door opened and one of the employees came out carrying his lunch. I had an idea. "Come on, you two. Let's go check something out."

I went up to the employee door and tried it. It was unlocked. Peeking inside, I recognized the hallway that I had gone down with Purple Hair Girl. The ducks and I made our way down the hall. When we got to the door of the equipment room, I paused and listened. I looked down at my companions. They looked back at me and waggled their tail feathers.

Twisting the knob, luck was with us. It was unlocked, too. I really need to talk to Corrie about the security of this place. Once we were inside, I flipped on the lights and shut the door behind us.

Everything was exactly where it had been the last time I was here. The racks of bows, the tubs of arrows, the golf clubs. There was only one thing that I was interested in, and it was right next to the door. The ducks, on the other hand, had a different idea. They waddled down the center aisle and disappeared behind the row of football pads. *Do ducks have a sense of smell?* I wondered. I wrinkled my nose at the sweaty pads and followed the birds.

A muffled crash followed by loud frantic quacking reached me before I could turn the corner. Harvey lay on his back, paddling like mad in the middle of a pile of pool noodles. Of course, they would find water toys! "You two are going to get us caught," I whispered as I righted the duck and picked up the noodles. "Come on, let's go back."

To my surprise, they listened. We walked between the shelves and I could see the long, black box partially hidden under the shelving by the door. I leaned down and slid it out. A small sticker angled across the lid, reading "Samples enclosed." I lifted the lid and saw arrows, nestled in foam padding, in alternating directions. They were black and had neon yellow fletching. There was space for six arrows, but half of the foam indentations were empty. Corrie had said that only six of the designer arrows had been made. And I'd seen them in Lucy's trunk!

Hearing voices in the hall, I quickly replaced the lid, slid the box under the shelf, and turned out the lights. Just like the night before in the boathouse, it was pitch black. The only light was seeping through the crack under the door. The voices receded and I opened the door a tiny bit. I watched two employees in their matching polo shirts walk toward the reception desk.

When the coast was clear, I led the ducks back the way we had come, out the door, and straight into Corrie. "What do you think you are doing?" Her face was the color of my famous Honey Sweet apples.

Chapter 23

"Taking a tour?" I said. I side-stepped around Corrie and walked to my golf cart.

Corrie stomped after me. However, Peeper and Harvey would have none of it. They started quacking and peeping and biting at her ankles. "Call them off!" she yelled, walking backward into a bush. She looked a little like a stranded turtle. I just stood and watched.

As soon as the ducks saw that Corrie wasn't going anywhere, they waddled calmly over to the cart and hopped in. "Nice work," I said.

We rounded the building and were headed out to the street when I saw two vehicles I recognized. One was a small green nondescript number with mismatched wheels. Parked right next to it was a giant, lifted black truck. Interesting.

I swung the golf cart in a wide arc and found a space near the front doors. I hopped out and headed into the lobby, followed by four small webbed feet. Directly opposite the front door was the weight room. The wall facing the lobby was made of glass, while the rest of the walls were mirrored. Loud music was pumping in the room and I could see Lucy doing bicep curls. I walked closer to the window and looked in.

Most of the people in the weight room were of average height, but there were a few that were pretty tall. I looked from person to person, trying to imagine each of them standing in the doorway of the boathouse in silhouette.

Hearing a commotion behind me, I turned just in time to see Harvey half-waddling, half-hopping across the floor with Purple Hair Girl hot on his tail. "Give me back my earbuds!" she was yelling.

I chased after the mallard and managed to scoop him up. I pulled the earbuds from the duck's bill and handed them back to the receptionist. "I'm so sorry. He's a bit of a... collector." I smiled at the girl, who grabbed the earbuds and headed back to the front counter.

I followed her and said, "Do you mind if I ask you a question?"

The girl started putting the earbuds in her ears. She paused and said, "What?"

"Who all has access to the equipment room? I know you let me in the other day. Were you doing me a special favor, or is it just open to anyone?" I put the squirming duck on the ground and leaned on the counter.

Purple Hair Girl sighed and glanced around the lobby. "Don't tell anyone I did that, K? I could lose my job. Only staff is supposed to be in there. Employees have to come up here and sign out the key and everything."

I pointed to a clipboard lying next to the phone. "Is that the clipboard? Is that the only key?"

The girl was starting to get fidgety. "Yes and no. Yes, that's the clipboard. No, that's not the only key. There are three keys. This one, the night custodian has one, and of course, Corrie has one. Why do you want to know?"

"Have you checked the room lately? It's a mess, and it doesn't seem like anyone is keeping it locked, either." I raised my eyebrows.

Purple Hair Girl jumped out of her seat. "Not again." She took off down the hall and checked the door. "You've got to be kidding me!" she screeched when she found that I was right. While she was away from the desk, I might or might not have taken a quick peek at the names on the clipboard. And learned exactly nothing.

"Come on, guys," I said. "Nothing more to learn here." I led the way out of the building.

"I think we should check in with Chief Ellis," I said. The ducks were strangely quiet. Then I noticed that Harvey was holding something in his bill again. Sighing, I pulled over and took the hair tie away from the duck. "You are something else, Harvey," I said, giving him a pat on the head.

At the town hall, I tried to convince my two companions that I would be fine on my own. It was the police department, after all. Of course, they paid no attention to me and walked right into the building. The desk sergeant took one look at the three of us and picked up the phone.

Chief Ellis laughed when he came to the lobby. "I thought he was pulling my leg," he said. "'Granny Appleton and two ducks are here to see you,' he said. I didn't believe him." The chief pulled me into a side hug and said, "There's never a dull moment with you around. Come on back to my office."

After the usual banter about the weather and family and an explanation about my feathered friends, I leaned forward and said, "Buck, I think there's some monkey business going on here. Something isn't adding up."

Buck leaned forward and raised his eyebrows. "What do you mean?"

"I know that I told you that the arrow I found at Earl's farm was Lucy Cantana's, but now I'm not so sure."

The chief leaned back in his chair. "Go on."

"The arrow in question only LOOKS like Lucy's."

"Interesting." Buck was staring at the books on his bookcase.

I huffed, "Are you even listening, Buck. If you think Lucy is the arsonist, I think you are wrong. All of her arrows are accounted for. I saw them myself. The arrow that started the fire is a fake. A look-alike."

Buck pulled his chair up to the desk and leaned his elbows on it. "I'm listening. We've already talked to Lucy. She has an alibi for that night. But, we do know that Lucy had a motive. She's trying to start her own business, but Earl's been spreading rumors about her. She was at the Pointe of No Return that night. Along with everyone else in town. You were there, too, weren't you?"

"We were all celebrating Lucy's victory. Until that jerk Nick spoiled everything, that is. By the way, were you aware that he THREATENED Earl that night?"

Buck's eyebrows went up. "Really? That's news to me. Our officers are still interviewing everyone who was there that night. Would you mind putting that into a statement for me?"

"Couldn't you just consider it an anonymous tip?" I asked. "I also have another piece of evidence for you. But before I give it to you, I would like to see the arrow to confirm my suspicions. Trade?" I gave him my best smile.

"Withholding information is a crime, you know," Buck said.

I just sat, smiling.

"I could have you arrested."

More smiling.

"Fine. I don't have the real thing right here. That's locked up in our evidence room, but I do have photos. Will that do?" Buck pulled out one of his desk drawers and withdrew a file. He took out some 8 x 10 glossy photos and slid them across the desk.

I grabbed them up and studied them. I shuffled through the stack until I came to some that showed close-ups around the fletching and nock.

"Aha!" I exclaimed. The ducks had settled under my chair and started making noises like crazy. "Sorry!"

Buck came around the desk and sat in the chair next to me. "What aha?" he asked. "This is one of Lucy's arrows. We're sure of it."

I pointed at the nock. "What do you see?"

"A place to hook the arrow to the bowstring." Buck shrugged his shoulders.

"Anything else?"

Buck took the photo from me and studied it. "Nope. Just an arrow shaft and the end part."

"It's called a nock," I informed him. "And you're right. There's nothing there. On Lucy's arrows, she has her initials inscribed. Did you even *look* at her arrows? I did. They are in a long, black box, and all of them are accounted for."

"Was that your piece of evidence?" Buck asked.

"That's one of them," I said. "You might want to look in the equipment room at the rec center. There just *might* be another long, black box hiding under a shelf. It could be worth your time to check it out." I fished under the edge of my wig. "That, and also this little note that I found in the market. At least two people out there know what happened to Earl. Quinn and I almost caught them, but your night patrol scared one of them off before we could hear the conversation."

Buck looked at the note and sputtered, "What! When... why... you..."

"We were hiding in the boathouse and one of them had a key to get in. They are both tall and muscular, but we couldn't tell if either of them was male or female. It was very dark last night."

Before Buck could say another word, I stood up and took my leave, the ducks waddling calmly after me.

Chapter 24

Back in my kitchen, I rolled out another batch of pie dough. The blueberries were in a saucepan on the stove, bubbling merrily in their sugary bath.

With each roll I made, I thought about what was missing. I went to stir the sweet syrupy filling, replaying the evening of the fire in my mind. It had seemed like the entire community had tried to cram into the restaurant and congratulate Lucy. The manager had opened champagne and everything. I remembered the music being loud and people dancing. Earl doing the two-step with Divina. He had even slow danced with me.

I had never seen him that relaxed. I wondered if it had something to do with his daughter being home. I smiled when I tried to imagine how their reunion had been. I mean the part before she told him about her marriage. Wiping a tear from my eye, I poured the filling into the pie shells and popped them into the oven.

As soon as the pies were on the cooling rack, I decided to head over to the Foxman place to check on the animals. With Earl at the hospital with Judy, I wanted to make sure the animals were taken care of. And maybe have another look around.

I hung up my apron and left a note for Quinn. The sharp creak of the back screen door brought the ducks running to take a ride.

Everything at Earl's looked just as I had left it the day before. There was no sign of the gold-colored car I'd seen in the driveway, and Earl's beat-up yellow truck wasn't there. Old Mutt was still in the yard. He barked a few times, but when he realized it was me, he quit. I checked his food and water dishes. They were half full. He nuzzled my hand and completely ignored the ducks.

There were several buildings surrounding the large patch of gravel at the back of the house. Besides the barn, there was a metal shop with two garage doors, the grain silo for corn, and a shed. I went to the shed and peeked in. It was empty. The grain silo next to it wouldn't be used to shelter animals, but I checked it anyway in the name of being thorough. *I'm looking out for the animals*, I told myself. The ducks found a few kernels of corn to munch on. They poked their heads into every crack and crevice.

Next to the silo were several pens. I found the ewe and her lambs that I had helped escape from the barn. Mama was contentedly chewing her cud while her fat lambs butted her side as they took a snack break. They didn't look any worse for their harrowing adventure in the burning barn. The rest of the pens had a few sheep in them, but they all had food and water, so I moved on after watching them for a few minutes.

I went to the shop next. This building was what everyone called a pole barn. It wasn't a barn but was constructed of wooden poles placed vertically in the ground for framing. A concrete floor was poured, then large sheets of corrugated metal were used to build the walls and roof. This one was light blue in color and had a white roof. Besides the two garage doors, there was a walk-in door on the side.

I tried the door. It was unlocked. I stepped inside and found a light switch on the wall. Large overhead fluorescent lights kicked on and started making a buzzing sound. It was rather eerie in the otherwise silent space. It smelled faintly of oil and gasoline. The area close to the door had a cement floor. There was a long counter top that extended clear to the back. The walls in this area were covered with transportation memorabilia. There were all sorts of metal signs from gas stations. An old-fashioned gas pump stood in a corner.

Earl had added a second story to this half of the shop out of two-by-fours and plywood. To me, it looked like what people were calling a 'man cave'. The vast majority of the large building, however, had dirt floors and was filled with farm equipment. I recognized Earl's big red and white tractor as well as a cultivator and a disc harrow.

With the ducks at my heels, I walked the length of the shop. Earl was a very organized farmer. Everything had a peg on the wall, a space on a shelf, or a container on the floor. All the equipment was lined up perfectly.

I was impressed. My own husband had been a 'toss it in the corner because I'm in a hurry' kind of guy. I was always having to pick up after him in the house. I generally stayed out of his space in the outbuildings on our farm. Now that he was gone, I was slowly cleaning out and organizing those buildings, but sometimes it was too painful when memories came flooding back.

Seeing nothing out of place, and no animals to tend to, I turned around and headed to the door. "Peeper, Harvey, come on, you guys," I called. The ducks were nowhere to be seen. I walked back towards the tractor. I could hear little peeps coming from behind it. As I walked toward the sound, something caught my eye. Next to the tractor was a fertilizer spreader. It was halfway disassembled, with the parts scattered around. I stepped over the pieces to the back wall. There was a large black patch in the dirt floor that didn't belong there. I knelt down next to it and studied it. With my heart in my throat, I put my finger out and touched the edge. When I pulled my hand back, my fingertip was covered in a slick black substance. I sniffed it. Oil. I let out the breath I hadn't even noticed I was holding.

I walked back outside and was standing there, studying the barn, when Earl's truck drove into the yard. He parked next to my golf cart and stepped out.

"Just what do you think you're doin' here, Granny?" he said, walking around to the back of the truck and lowering the tailgate.

I hurried over to the truck. "I just wanted to check in on your animals, since you were at the hospital."

"That's mighty kind of you, but we don't need no help. You just head on home and tend to your own place," Earl said. He grabbed a large bag of dog food and lifted it to his shoulder. He walked to the house and slammed the door behind him.

I just stood there, staring after him. Part of me felt guilty for being on his property without permission, but part of me was angry at Earl for dismissing me like that. As I was debating about giving him a piece of my mind, I felt something rubbing my leg. It was an orange and white tabby cat. I reached down and absently rubbed its sleek fur.

Letting out a big sigh, I decided to head home. Nothing good would come of me talking to Earl. He never listened to anyone, just waited for them to stop speaking so he could say his piece. Calling the ducks, I went to the golf cart and climbed in. Peeper waddled out of some tall weeds near the shop area, followed by Harvey. They were quite the pair. I smiled at the contrast between the big white duck and the little dark one. The blue ring of feathers around Harvey's neck shone in the sunlight. I noticed that he had found another treasure.

"Not again, Harvey. One of these days you are going to choke on something. Give it here."

When the ducks hopped into the cart, I wrestled Harvey's beak open and removed his find. It was just a small piece of trash. A small cellophane wrapper. Wait a minute. I held it to my nose. It smelled like mint. The sound it made as I handled it reminded me of sitting in the darkened boathouse, listening to someone sitting in the lawn chair. And it reminded me of sitting in Corrie Wagner's office, watching her eat a mint. My heart was in my throat as the pieces started falling into place.

I reached for my cell phone, only to realize that I'd left it on the kitchen counter again. I quickly released the brake and gunned the little cart down the driveway, tucking the wrapper in my pocket as I drove.

I slowed when I came around the corner and saw a big blue work truck sitting there. Corrie Wagner's truck. No one was in it. Glancing around the farmyard, I wondered where my two dogs had gone off to. They were probably taking a nap under one of the apple trees in the orchard. Figures. I made my way slowly up to the back door and opened it. The familiar squeak jarred my brain.

Corrie was sitting at my kitchen table, a half-eaten slice of blueberry pie sitting in front of her.

"Hello, Granny," she said, in a voice that would chill a glass of sun tea on a hot summer day. "I thought I'd come by and have a chat. You don't mind, do you? I know that you like to drop by unannounced and bother people, so I didn't think you would. Have a seat." She indicated the chair across from her as if this was her office. "This pie's not half bad, by the way. Could have used a touch more lemon juice, but that's just my opinion."

I slowly pulled out the chair and scanned the counters as I sat down.

"Looking for this?" Corrie asked, holding out my cell phone. "You left it next to the note you wrote for Quinn." She tossed the phone across the kitchen, into the sink, which was full of soapy water where I had been soaking my baking dishes. "Oops." Corrie put her hand to her mouth in mock horror.

"You really didn't need to leave Quinn a note. She won't be coming home any time soon. Someone broke into the boathouse and vandalized the controls for that fancy sprinkler pump. Probably someone looking for that expensive copper wiring to sell. It's going to take her a long time to fix that."

I stood up quickly and pulled my phone out of the cool water. Reaching for a towel, I dried it off the best I could. The screen was all foggy and kept glitching. Quinn would know how to fix it.

I walked to the cupboard. "Well, I might as well have a piece of pie, too, then." I pulled out a small plate and cut a slice. "Would you like another one?" The pie server shook as I tried to put the piece on my plate. My mind was racing a million miles an hour. Where was this conversation going?

"Nah, but a cup of coffee might be nice. But only if you are going to make one for yourself. I wouldn't want to be a bother." Corrie drummed her fingers on the table and leaned back. I glanced in her direction. The smile on Corrie's face reminded me of the Cheshire cat from Alice in Wonderland. I had never liked that cat.

As I filled the coffee maker, Corrie said, "You know, Granny, I had an interesting visit from the police today."

"Oh?" I didn't know what else to say. I tried to keep my expression neutral.

"They had a warrant to search my equipment room." More table drumming.

I had to hand it to Buck. He didn't let the moss grow under his feet.

"It seems to me that you were in that area earlier. What were you doing there, Granny? Planting evidence so that my receptionist would get arrested? Covering your tracks? Trying to lay the blame on someone else so that no one knows it was you who set that fire? You want Earl's land for yourself, don't you?"

I took two mugs out of the cupboard by the sink and set them down, keeping my back to Corrie. I filled the mugs and brought them to the table. "Can't plant something that was already there, Corrie."

"Bold words, Granny, bold words." Corrie pulled her mug to her and sipped. Then she reached for the sugar bowl and added a heaping spoonful. As she stirred, she asked, "What exactly did you find in there that you thought the police would be interested in?"

"You were the one who custom-designed those arrows for Lucy. She told me that only six arrows were made. Yet, I found another box of matching arrows in the equipment room. Interesting. I'll bet if the police search your computer, they will find the invoice for those extra arrows, too."

"So? She could have lied to you. Ever think of that?" Corrie put the coffee down and glared at me.

I put my own mug down and nodded. "Good point, Corrie. Except for one tiny detail. Lucy had another company put her initials on her arrows. The ones in the equipment room aren't hers. They are yours, aren't they? But why are you trying to frame her for the fire at Earl's barn?"

Corrie's face was getting red, and that vein in her forehead had popped out. "That good for nothing tramp was horning in on Nick. She knows that I'm interested in him, but she won't back off. Burning down Earl's barn and having her go down for it takes care of two of my biggest problems. Earl gets to stay busy minding his own business for a change, and Nick won't be interested in a jailbird." She crossed her arms smugly.

I giggled. I couldn't help myself. It just slipped out. The more I thought about it, the funnier it got. The giggles turned into guffaws and I grabbed a napkin to wipe my eyes. It took me a few minutes to get control. Even then, a stray snicker would come out.

"What is so funny?" Corrie had this look on her face like she thought I'd finally lost my marbles.

I wiped my eyes one more time and took a sip of my coffee. When I was fairly sure that I had my composure back, I cleared my throat and said, "Your infatuation with that walking ham bone has blinded you to an important fact. There's a reason that Lucy hangs around with Nick, and it's not because she wants him for her boyfriend. He's her BROTHER, you dolt."

Corrie slapped her palm on the table, causing the dishes to jump. "You're lying!"

"I'm sure if you check his rec center membership card, he has her listed as his next of kin."

Corrie stood up suddenly, sending the kitchen chair flying backward and crashing to the floor. "She was in the way, just like Earl, just like you are." She reached behind her back and her hand came up holding a small silver pistol. "Get up, Granny. We're going to go for a walk."

My first reaction was shock. To be confronted in your own kitchen with a gun? Over pie? Who does that? Then I narrowed my eyes. What was this crazy loon capable of? Slowly, I got to my feet and walked to the door. I held my tongue. It's not wise to argue with an unstable person holding a firearm.

The screen door gave its customary squeak as we walked outside. Across the yard, the big white duck came running, followed by the dark mallard. They headed towards the golf cart, ready for a ride. I paused, glancing over my shoulder at Corrie. She was glaring at the ducks. "I'll take care of those two next."

She shoved my shoulder. "To the barn. You are about to have yourself an accident," she said, gesturing with the gun.

I started across the yard. "An accident? What are you talking about?" I moved stiffly, trying to stall.

Corrie gave my shoulder another shove and I stumbled. "Accidents happen on farms all the time. Barns are dangerous places. Lots of sharp tools and things, you know. Faulty wiring, stuff like that. Earl was supposed to have an accident, too." We reached the barn and Corrie used one hand to push the heavy door open. It took barely any effort on her part, where I had to use both hands and practically throw my back out to get the thing to move.

We walked into the cool interior and Corrie looked around. She pointed to the ladder lying off to one side. "Set it up and start climbing, old lady."

I gulped and shook my head. "I don't like heights," I said.

"You want to try running? I've won several moving target pistol competitions. I wouldn't mind a little action practice. Get moving!" She took a step closer to me and raised the gun. I scrambled to get the ladder.

Setting the ladder next to the large stack of hay under the mezzanine, I started climbing, expecting to feel the searing heat of a bullet in my back at every step. I was almost at the top when I heard a commotion. I turned and saw Peeper, bill wide open, wings flapping wildly, come running through the door. Harvey, dragging his injured wing, was right beside her, his long neck stretched out in front of him.

Corrie screamed and yelled, "Get away from me!" She kicked at the ducks with one foot and started climbing up the ladder behind me. Her foot made contact with Peeper's chest and sent her backward into the straw scattered around the outside of their makeshift pen. Harvey was doing his best to strike with his good wing and nip at her ankles. The ladder was shaking and I was holding on for dear life. I wasn't kidding when I said I was afraid of heights.

Peeper wiggled and rocked until she got herself upright. Then she came right back at Corrie. Out of nowhere, Harvey took flight and managed to fly right up into Corrie's face. She lost her balance and fell sideways off the ladder, firing the gun as she did so. She grabbed for one of the hay bales that were stacked close by. She managed to hook her hand under the baling twine, but as she hung there, the bale tipped and slid off the stack, taking Corrie with it.

I felt a sharp pain in my left shoulder. Glancing down, I saw blood seeping through my shirt. I gripped the ladder even more tightly and closed my eyes. My ears were ringing from the gunshot and I started to feel very dizzy. When I regained my equilibrium, I looked down and saw that Corrie was lying on the ground, partially under the bale of hay. Both ducks were sitting on top of the bale. I think they were smiling at me.

Taking a deep breath, I slowly and carefully made my way down the ladder. I knelt down next to Corrie and felt for a pulse. It was there, but she wasn't going to be doing any strenuous workouts for a while. One of her legs was twisted in a very unnatural position.

Harvey had a very loud quacking session and Peeper chimed in. "Great job, you two," I said. "You probably just saved my life." My left arm was numb and I knew that I needed to get help for both of us, and quickly.

Reaching into Corrie's pocket, I found her cell phone and dialed 911. I sat there, putting pressure on my arm and wondered what would push a person over the edge to where they would harm another human being. And think that would help their situation.

As I heard sirens in the distance, I closed my eyes and allowed the darkness to take over.

Chapter 25

A week later, I was back in the kitchen, whipping up one of my signature apple crumble pies. I was still a little sore and had to favor my left arm as I rolled out the crust, but other than that, I was none the worse for the wear. I was tired of being fussed over and ready to get my life back to normal.

While the pie baked, I sat at the table to give my arm a rest. The doctor had told me that he'd had a tough time fishing the bullet out of my shoulder and that I was lucky that it had been a small-caliber weapon. I leafed through a magazine, not really seeing what was on the pages. I was still trying to wrap my head around everything that had happened.

The timer went off and I put the pie on the cooling rack. I went to my bedroom and selected a short, curly brown wig to wear. I put it on and arranged it until it looked perfect. I put on my walking shoes and grabbed my market basket. I put in the warm pie and went out the back door.

Harvey quacked at me from the front seat of the golf cart. Peeper blinked at me with her big liquid eyes. I set the basket on the floorboards and we headed down the dirt road.

Parked in front of the Foxman house was a beat-up green car with shiny new tires. I pulled in next to it. The ducks and I made our way through the gate and found Judy and Lucy sitting on the patio, drinking iced tea.

"Granny! What a surprise," Judy said. "Lucy and I were just talking about you." She gave me a hug and motioned for me to sit with them. She picked up a pitcher dripping with condensation and poured me a glass.

Lucy eyed the ducks and said, "Don't let those things near me. Every time I see them, I end up losing my car keys." She patted her pocket protectively.

The ducks settled under my chair and closed their eyes. "I think you are safe, for now." Holding up the basket, I said, "I brought a pie. If you have some plates, Judy, it would go great with this wonderful iced tea."

Soon we were enjoying warm pie and good conversation. Judy was laughing and smiling. I was happy to see that there was a natural glow to her skin, instead of the pallor that she'd had in the hospital. Lucy was relaxed and seemed to be enjoying herself. Not nearly as uptight as she usually was.

Judy shared some news. "Dad and I went to see an attorney the other day. They are helping me get a divorce from that scum, Ivan. He really did put all that sleeping medicine in my drink. I think he was trying to drug me when I refused to help him. He wanted to talk Dad into signing the contract with his company and have the farm turned into a housing development. He thought if he made it look like I was trying to commit suicide, Dad would break and want to get rid of the place. Can you imagine?" She waved her hand to indicate the rolling green farmland that stretched in front of them.

I nodded solemnly. "The first time I saw him when you and Earl were in the refreshment tent, I knew he looked familiar. He paid me a call last year and tried to buy my place. I laughed him off the property. I'm guessing that when he visited Earl, he somehow learned about your falling out and he tracked you down. What a snake. Using you to get what he wanted." I shook my head.

"Dad tried to warn me about him, but I was too stupid to listen," Judy said. There was a catch in her voice and she looked away suddenly. "Those stubborn genes sure do run deep in our family." She laughed softly. "Ivan left me there to die and hasn't called or texted or anything."

"He was my prime suspect for the barn fire," I said. "He sure had the motive."

Lucy spoke up. "People around town thought that I did it, too. Even the police. I came within a hair's breadth of being put in the slammer for it."

I took my last bite of pie and scraped up the crumbs. Using my fork for a pointer, "That's right. Earl was trying to convince everyone in town that you were pushing drugs. You were madder than a wet hen about it, too."

"My brother's the one who does that, not me," Lucy said. She clenched her fists tightly. "He got picked up for selling illegal muscle enhancers just after you ended up in the hospital, Granny. I knew he was up to something hinky when he asked to come and stay with me. That big new truck, all his fancy clothes. All I wanted to do was grow some hops." She looked at Judy and grinned. Judy was grinning, too.

I looked at them each in turn. "I'm missing something here. What's going on?"

Judy clapped her hands. "Well, you see, Granny, some good has come out of all of this mess, after all. Dad and I were at the Pointe of No Return one day for lunch. Lucy gave us a tour of the brewery equipment and showed us how micro brews were made. Dad realized he'd made a mistake and a partnership was born!

We have to rebuild the barn anyway, so we are going to convert it into a micro-brewery. Lucy can grow her own hops and other grains right here and that way the costs are lower and we can control the quality."

I looked at Lucy. "You must be really good at sweet-talking. I don't think anyone, ever, has convinced Earl Foxman to change his mind. Congratulations! Here's to dreams coming true." I raised my glass. "A toast! To the new entrepreneurs in town. May your venture be successful."

The women clinked glasses and smiled at each other.

"I just wish that snake, Corrie, wouldn't have taken all my money," Lucy said. "She had rigged the competition so that the winnings went mostly to her, for 'administrative costs.'" She used her fingers to make air quotes.

"So, that's what she meant about reading the fine print," I mused. "Well, she won't be enjoying that money where she's going. I'm sure that the board of directors will sort it out." I stood up. "I'd better be getting home. Unlike you, I have animals that will be clamoring for their dinner soon." Lucy and Judy followed me and the ducks out of the yard to the golf cart.

Judy gave me a hug, being careful not to squeeze my injured arm. "Thank you for all your help with everything," she said. "I'm so glad to be back home. I can't believe I wanted to be away from all this." The sun was setting and had colored the sky a brilliant shade of orange.

I climbed into the golf cart and backed up. Then I pulled forward and held out my hand to Lucy. "You might want to find a better place to keep these," I said, handing over a set of keys.

"Those darn ducks!" Lucy laughed.

Zucchini Pie

Recipe given to me by my mother-in-law, Nancy Beaton (given to her by Lucy Yates).

Ingredients:

1 cup zucchini – peeled, cooked, mashed, and cooled

1 cup sugar

1 cup evaporated milk

1 egg

2 tablespoons flour

2 tablespoons melted butter

1 teaspoon vanilla

cinnamon

Preheat oven to 425 degrees. Place all ingredients into a blender together, or mix by hand very well. Pour mixture into unbaked pie shell. Sprinkle top with cinnamon. Bake at 425 degrees for 30 minutes or until done.

I'm thinking that a dollop of whipped cream would be tasty on top!

More Pie?

Granny would love to bake more pies for you! And I would love to write more about her adventures. Would you consider doing something for her?

Reviews are like slices of pie to an author. Would you write an honest review about Duck Down on Amazon? It would mean a lot!

About the Author

Missy Tarantino is a teacher in Northern Colorado. She works with children who are just learning English and come from all over the world.

When she isn't in the classroom, you'll find her out having adventures. She is an amateur race car driver and loves going fast on autocross courses.

You can connect with me on:

https://www.missytarantino.com

https://www.facebook.com/missywritesbooks

Subscribe to my newsletter:

https://landing.mailerlite.com/webforms/landing/n4c0t4

Also by Missy Tarantino

The Feather Forecast
When a storm of epic proportions hits Paisley Pointe, forcing its citizens indoors, the business alliance comes up with a creative idea to help banish the blues. But when strange lights start showing up in the gloomy skies, Granny knows that something has to be done to keep her community from turning into a ghost town. Will she be able to track down the source before everyone flees under threat of alien abduction?

Robber Ducky

A Founder's Day celebration gone wrong. A klepto duck with an eye for shiny objects. Does Granny have what it takes to bring down the thief?

Granny is focused on training for her first 5k race. Telling her she can't do something is a guarantee she's going to succeed. When she is bowled over during the race by a jewelry thief, Granny will do everything she can to run him down.

Getting the brush-off from law enforcement pushes Granny to step in and get nosy. She comes up with a plan to get up close and personal with the investigation. But with so many suspects, will she be able to weed out the thief?

Robber Ducky is the third duckumentary in the Granny Appleton Cozy Mystery series. If you like reading about quirky, wig-wearing grannies and rescue animals with cute personalities, then this is the book for you.

Buy Robber Ducky today and give the jewel thief their own pair of bracelets.

Quacking the Case
A felon on the loose. Fear in the community. Will Granny fall victim or save the day?

It's harvest time on Granny's farm and she's up to her elbows in apples. When the chief of police tells Granny there's a convict in the area, she shrugs it off. But when Granny realizes she isn't alone in the orchard, she sees things differently.

Granny keeps her head on a swivel and a shotgun nearby. A light in the orchard at night confirms her suspicions. Will Granny catch the felon before he takes her out?

Quacking the Case is the fourth book in the Granny Appleton series. If you like cozy mysteries, then you'll love this one.

Buy the book today and help rid the world of a bad apple.

www.ingramcontent.com/pod-product-compliance
Lightning Source LLC
LaVergne TN
LVHW050650100826
845148LV00011B/2062

* 9 7 9 8 9 8 6 0 4 1 4 1 4 *